Once We Were Heroes

Once We Were Heroes

Henry Lewi

Bridge House

British Library Cataloguing in Publication Data
A Record of this Publication is available from the British
Library

ISBN 978-1-914199-82-0

This edition published 2024 by Bridge House Publishing
Manchester, England

Contents

Introduction

I started writing some of these short stories during the National Lockdowns that began in 2020, and some may reflect that sense of isolation and anxiety that enveloped us all.

During that time the public were consumed with interest as to where the virus had come from, was it manufactured? Was it extra-terrestrial? Had we slipped into an alternative universe? Who knew?

Many of these stories were written as an escape from the then everyday lockdown life of online shopping, gardening and television that occupied us all, and some were written as a "What If?"

Enjoy the improbable or is it the probable?

The Gods Do Tesco

One Monday morning Zeus the chief God announced that the stocks of ambrosia on Mount Olympus were running dangerously low. "We've got to find a way of restocking, but mankind has lost respect for the old gods and won't make any more Ambrosia or provide us offerings of wine."

His daughter Athena the goddess of wisdom replied, "I blame the state of the Greek economy and the EU. The Greeks don't have two euros to rub together and impose additional taxes on the wine they make."

"It's not just that," replied Apollo. "In the interests of diversity and equality, one group of gods can't be singled out for preferential treatment. I was chatting to Thor, and he tells me that they are treated much better in Norway outside the EU. We're not looked on kindly as we have more male Gods than female, so our EU Major Deity Grant is being slashed."

"Right," said Zeus' wife, Hera. "We've got to do some shopping. You Apollo, and your sister Artemis, get yourselves down to Tesco, as I hear they've a two for one offer on honey and ambrosia. Take the Golden Chariot, you can park it in mother and child's bay, but remember to turn off the Rising Sun option when you park up."

"Mum! Really? Do I have too? I've got a date with that Norwegian dish "Balder the Beautiful" this afternoon. Can't Ares go? He's got no major wars that he's got to be at."

Later that afternoon Apollo and Ares entered the Tesco Store dressed in their finest white Togas edged in Gold.

It was sheer madness; the store was crowded with people obviously humans who were running hither and thither with no respect being shown for the two gods that walked amongst them!

"What in Hades name is going on?" said Ares.

"Look people are running around with armfuls of toilet paper and pasta."

"Dunno," said a sullen Apollo – truth be told he didn't like Tesco; he was more a Fortnum's kind of god. "Maybe those Roman gods have inflicted some kind of plague like they did a few years ago, what did they call it? Oh Yeah Black Death or something like that."

"Nah," said Ares. "That wasn't the Romans; it was that bunch of Indian Gods that sent it West. Anyway, that was because I stole the idea of the longbow from them and gave it to that English guy – what's his name Ed, Eddy or Edward something? Besides it was nearly 700 years ago!"

Apollo's phone pinged, and looking at it he said, "There's a WhatsApp message on the 'Major Deity Group Chat' from someone called Monkey."

"Who's he?" he asked no one in particular.

"Chinese God of Mischief," answered a red-faced slightly overweight man carrying a huge pile of toilet rolls. "A bit like that bloke Loki who's just gone all Hollywood with the Marvel Studios!"

"Thanks," said Apollo. "Seems like he's sent this message out advising us that he'd got some viral infection from some Pangolins he was looking after for that Mexican mate of his, Yum something or other, who's gone on a cruise to the Far East, and he won't be able to meet up with everybody at the annual Ragnarök festival."

"Where's it this year?" asked Ares.

"Milan," I think replied Apollo, "but with all this toilet roll epidemic they're talking about cancelling it."

Sadly, the shelves were empty of honey and ambrosia and the Tesco store manager had no idea when the next delivery would take place.

"It's in the Lap of the Gods," he stated staring directly

at Apollo, "You're the god of Medicine go and have a word with that guy COBRA, who seems to run the Government, and sort it out will you!"

"What a jerk," said Apollo as they left the store. "What are we going to do now? Any ideas?"

"Why don't we try Waitrose? A much better class of store and customer, they're bound to have ambrosia at least – though we'll have to pay extra; they don't do a two for one deal!" said Ares.

First published on CaféLit 20 July 2020

Papa Jean

In the hot sticky night, they found his twentieth victim and they knew Papa Jean had returned. They found the body of a young woman behind the Café du Monde on the banks of the Mississippi.

Today the good folks of New Orleans would not be having their beignets. The FBI profiler didn't believe in Voodoo mystery and refused to listen to the tales from the NOPD or the locals.

They told of stories of a killer that had lived amongst them for the last 200 years. They talked of a curse.

They spoke of a murderer that had arrived from the old island of Santa Domingo. They spoke of a dead French Slaver seeking vengeance.

They told of how when the summer nights were hot, Papa Jean appeared and killed, always leaving his mark.

The young FBI agent dismissed the stories. "Just a myth," he said, adding, "The killer is copying the crimes of this so-called Papa Jean."

"Go read de story," replied the Police Lieutenant in his N'awlins accent. "Dis is my second cycle of killings I've witnessed, de last one was twenty years ago; de bodies were all over de place and stopped when dey got to thirty, we never got eem. Me Pappy was in de force also. He told me he was involved in looking for Papa Jean also, and he says the killer came from de Slave Islands."

In the shadows the killer watched and listened. His profile occasionally lit up by the flickering lights of the police vehicles. He was tired. He needed a new body. This one he was using was worn out, modern life he thought, bad food, no exercise, too many cigarettes, he'll have to choose his next one carefully; maybe, that FBI guy would be ideal. He closed his eyes and probed the minds around him seeking the profiler's thoughts.

11

In the hot sultry night, he explored, he learnt the profiler was almost an Englishman that curious mix of a Bostonian brought up and educated in England. Time spent at Quantico, the experience in the field and the training in behavioural science. He was popular with both the NOPD and his FBI colleagues, he was healthy, and he was fit.

Oh! He was a vegetarian, Merde! Ça Marche pas. Bien, he thought. *Not for me, I'll watch.* He watched the sun came up.

He watched; he saw the shimmering image of Algiers Island across the water.

He watched, as the first ferry crossed to the Canal Street Ferry Port, as the ambulance took away the body, and as the Café du Monde workers opened a coffee stand for the police.

The heat rose from the ground as the sun heated it up and Algiers disappeared behind a haze.

He watched and remembered. He remembered the slaves arriving. He remembered the slave markets. He remembered the battle for New Orleans in '15, the fires that destroyed the shipyards in '62 and the old plantation houses in '95.

The humidity and heat were becoming uncomfortable and as he left the shadows and unobserved crossed Jackson Square and entered the Cabildo. The marbled floor of the Sala was as always cool and reassuring.

The portraits of the great and good of old New Orleans brought back memories of who he was, why he was, and where he had been.

He remembered when he had first arrived in '12.

The Cabildo then had served as the courthouse and centre of the N'Orleans Government.

Climbing to the next floor he wandered into the gallery devoted to the Battle of New Orleans of 1815. He stopped at a portrait of "Les Volontaires Francaise d'Orleans". He stared at the image of himself, Jean Baptiste St. Juste Honore in the second row, or who he had been then, 200 years ago.

He remembered. He recalled.

The slave revolt had begun on the Island of Santa Domingo in 1791.

For many years the leaders of the revolt murdered the Spanish, the French, and each other. They switched sides and allegiances at will. Jean Baptiste and his family-owned slaves and a sugar cane plantation in the north of the island. During his absence in Port au Prince, Toussaint Louverture and his men, burnt the plantation and murdered Jean Baptiste's family and their slaves during Louverture's "March of Freedom."

The island burnt as the sugar cane and coffee plantations were put to the torch. In retaliation Jean Baptiste led 300 slave and plantation owners, with French and Spanish militia on a "Ride of Death" across the Northern half of the island.

During one attack on a village of freed slaves, Jean Baptiste was faced by a young Creole woman, the voodoo princess known as *"ti se Marie"*, holding a small figurine in one hand and a white cockerel in the other standing in front of her burning hut.

"I curse you Jean Baptiste St. Juste Honore, I curse you and your family, to walk the earth in shame and death," she said.

Before Jean Baptiste could reach her, she bit off the head of the cockerel, doused the figurine with its blood, and threw both into the flames, even as he ran her through with his sabre.

Jean Baptiste had been cursed many times before. *What was the babbling of one more Creole witch worth?*

Jean Baptiste developed a hunger to kill that he needed to feed.

After the massacre of 1804 Jean Baptiste, like most of the French settlers, had to leave the island of Santa Domingo, and he travelled the islands, from Santa Domingo to Guadeloupe. From Guadeloupe to Jamaica, from Jamaica to Trinidad, helping to put down slave insurrections on behalf whichever group of owners paid him.

The hunger never left and was rarely satiated.

In 1812 he arrived aboard a slave transport at Algiers Island, hoping for a different life in the newly purchased US city of New Orleans. A new killing field had opened up, and now the enemy were the British who were waging war against the young country.

In the past two centuries he'd been able to wear new bodies like clothes. He knew how to change, but not the why of the change. His hunger now came in cycles: usually a single kill sufficed for months but every few years he had to feed on many "companions", always during the hot summer months.

After a summer killing cycle, he learnt he had to change. Sometimes he was tired, weary, and exhausted, and then he'd kill, and take a new body. As long as he could use his hands, eyes and mind he could move from body to body.

His thoughts were interrupted by a group of tourists. *Les Anglais; only they wear socks with their shorts and sandals.* He stepped back into the shadowed part of the salon. He watched, he listened, he waited. He felt the sharp edge of the blade in his pocket. He'd follow.

Their guide was a young pretty Creole woman who spoke with the Cajun patois. *Ah Chère, a companion you will be.*

Through the hot humid day, he shadowed her and the tourists, as they wandered through the French quarter.

As he stepped out to cross Basin Street to enter Treme-Lafitte he never saw the truck that hit him.

Waking up was a struggle; he couldn't breathe easily, couldn't move, or turn his head, and he couldn't speak.

"Cher," she said, bending over him, "c'est Marie. I'm finally en face with you again. I've followed and lost you all these years; I got close many times, but you changed. I knew it was you Jean Baptiste, you watching at the Café du Monde, you watching at the Cabildo.

"L'accident, me truck, broke your back; you can't move, you can't leave, you will hunger and remember the islands. Adieu Jean Baptiste St. Juste Honore."

Papa Jean could only lie there unable to move. He could move his eyes. He was paralyzed from the neck down. A tube in his throat was helping him breathe. He couldn't feed. His hunger grew. He couldn't move, he couldn't change and he couldn't leave. He could only remember.

He was alone, totally alone.

The Icing on the Cake

It was autumn 1948. The watery sunlight tried to pierce the smoke stained windows of the office in Praed Street London. The city was grey, the people were grey, and those buildings that remained intact were grey. The war was over but London was still showing signs of the damage it had sustained throughout the years of the Blitz and the V1 and V2 Rocket attacks; and now a new war was being waged. It was a war beneath the headlines, it was a war fought across Europe, it was a war of secrets, and the battlefield was everywhere.

In the offices of The Committee of Awareness, Knowledge and Enlightenment, Antoine Le Glaçage sat with his feet up on his desk blowing smoke rings towards the ceiling. He was bored, so bored; this was a far cry from his days of high adventure when he had served with the SOE – Churchill's "Baker Street Irregulars" who had wreaked havoc across Nazi Occupied Europe during the last war.

His friend and colleague the Oxford educated Count Andrey Kozcinski, once of Section II of the Polish Intelligence Bureau, was slumped in the office's solitary armchair doing *The Times Crossword.*

The Offices of The Committee of Awareness, Knowledge and Enlightenment had been acquired by the Ministry of Ag and Fish from its previous owner, a portly fifty-six year old who had left his wife and run off to Bognor Regis with his twenty-three year old secretary.

These Committee rooms, now known as "The CAKE" in Whitehall circles, housed that section of Military Intelligence responsible for "housekeeping": in simple terms the elimination of foreign agents active on British soil and those individuals likely to endanger the security of the United Kingdom.

A Colonel A.E. F. Farquarson led the department; a World War 1 Veteran who had spent the last war training the Stay Behinds, that ultra-secret section of the Home Guard, trained in the dark arts of warfare, ready to commit assassinations, disrupt troop movements and perform random acts of terror in the event of a German Invasion.

"Five down, 'wound my heart with a monotonous languor'," read out Count Andrey. "Eight letters," he added.

"Isn't that a line from *Chanson d'automne* by Verlaine?" replied Le Glaçage, who like the Count had read Classics at Oxford before the war. "Eight letters you say, could it be the poet's name itself?"

"No," replied Count Andrey. "Doesn't fit; one across definitely doesn't have a V."

The ringing of the telephone on Le Glaçage's desk disrupted the peace and tranquillity of the office, and picking up the receiver, Farquarson briefly asked the two men to step into his office.

Le Glaçage and the Count walked into Farquarson's office to be met by their boss and seated opposite him, at the chief's desk, was, what was now being called a Whitehall Mandarin, dressed in his black Jacket and pinstripe trousers.

"Take a seat Gentlemen," said the monocle wearing Farquarson. "Whitehall has initiated 'The CAKE Protocol', which means you two are now centre stage."

The Whitehall Mandarin now spoke for the first time: "The person of interest is a certain MP on the Intelligence Appropriations Sub Committee. His issues with drugs, alcohol and gambling have awakened the interest of the Russians who are now blackmailing him; of course, I need not tell you how important the details of the Intelligence Appropriations meetings can be to others in the Intelligence field."

The Mandarin opened his briefcase and removed a

manila folder, which he handed to Le Glaçage. "We don't invoke the CAKE Protocol unless it is absolutely necessary, and here are his details, a number of photographs, and his address here in London; he has a house in Bayswater. He spends the weekends at his country home in Suffolk. How you do it is up to you. Whatever happens we'll throw a D-Notice at the papers so there will be no publicity, but it must be done quickly; the appropriations committee is meeting next week to discuss the new arrangements of the Intelligence Services and we don't want that falling into unfriendly hands, do we?"

Four days later the *Times Obituary Column* reported the sudden death of the MP at his Suffolk home, with *The Times* adding that his constituents and members of the House of Commons would sorely miss him.

As Antoine Le Glaçage walked into Farquarson's office, the Chief said, "Well played Le Glaçage: no fuss, no publicity." And jokingly using the English translation of his surname added, "You really are the ICING on the CAKE."

The New Olympus Postcode: The Move

"I can't get a Home Delivery slot," moaned Zeus to his wife Hera and daughters Artemis and Athena. "I've tried all the stores including that one called Iceland used by Odin and Frigg. There's no option for a 'Major God Delivery' only for NHS staff and Carers – even Apollo as God of Medicine can't access that option as he's not employed by the NHS."

"This is totally unacceptable," cried Artemis. "Look at my hair. I urgently need some hair products at the very least – I had to borrow some shampoo from Medusa last week and look what that's done to me!" She slapped down two snakes on the top of her head that had been woken up by her shouting.

"I know, darling," replied Hera. "We're all having to suffer. You know I like to put honey on my Bran Flakes – us gods have to keep regular. Anyway," she turned to Zeus, "why can't we get a Home Delivery slot?"

"For a start they won't deliver to our Postcode; apparently OLY 8US is outside the delivery areas of all the major supermarkets, and Harrods and Fortnum's won't risk their vans driving up the side of Mount Olympus. I know we haven't spoken to Hippolyta and her bunch of Amazons for over a thousand years, but I've heard that they've set up a delivery business, maybe we can ask them to help us out."

"Dad, you're so out of it," said Athena. "Haven't you heard: both Hermes and Cousin Nike have set up their own online stores and delivery network? What about asking them or even sending a couple of the boys down to one of the supermarkets if you can get a 'click and collect' slot if it's that desperate."

"I'd love to," replied Zeus, "but that idiot Bacchus, as he now calls himself ever since he was in those Spaghetti Westerns, has smashed up the Golden Chariot when he and a bunch of nymphs were pissed out of their minds last week."

"Yes," said Hera staring at Zeus, "ever since you threw the Mechanic (she of course meant Vulcan), out of Mount Olympus, we haven't been able to fix anything. Look at the plumbing; it's atrocious. And where is he now? Living in some volcano in Cape Verde – wind Surfing!" She flounced out followed by her pet peacock.

"That's it! I'm done with this place," shouted Zeus as he threw a thunderbolt, which immediately fizzled out before it hit the ground. "Nothing works around here! Right, I'm calling my cousin Hestia. She's set up an Estate Agency with that Roman bloke Janus to find us a modern place to live preferably in London especially as the UK is now leaving the European Union!"

He looked at both Athena and Artemis. "In the meantime Athena and Artemis, get onto the Amazons and see if you can arrange for them to provide some sort of home delivery. Are they still using the Centaurs, or have they had a falling out with them as well? Anyway, get Ares to help; he always got on well with those ladies. I'm off to speak to Hestia."

Having spoken to both Hestia and Janus who ran a discrete property service for all the major deities, Zeus announced to the assembled gods: "Right, we're moving to London and I'm looking for somewhere on a hill with views over the city and Hestia has suggested Hampstead, Highgate and somewhere in Brent which is much cheaper but has stunning views over the whole of London."

"We'd prefer Hampstead," shouted out Apollo and Artemis together.

What can you do with twins thought Zeus.

"I'd prefer Knightsbridge," said Athena. "The shopping is so cool."

"St. James is my choice," said Ares. "All those military clubs within walking distance and Jermyn Street is where I get my jackets made."

"I really don't mind where, so long as the plumbing works and there's a big lawn for the peacocks, but I draw the line at penthouse flats!" muttered Hera.

"Look,' said Zeus, "we need a biggish place with off road parking, plenty of room for entertaining, somewhere on a hill and with good transport links, and plenty of shops nearby, and far enough away from those Russian oligarchs who have no respect for the old order. "Hold on," he continued, "I'm just going to take this call from Hestia."

"Right guys, Janus has found a brilliant property in Brent, Northwest London, on the top of a Hill between some place called Cricklewood and Neasden that's near Wembley, overlooking a park with amazing views over the whole city.

"I know, I know, it's not got the NW3 postcode, but Janus says we can buy the two adjoining properties and the total cost will still be less than a six-bed house in Hampstead. Just think: great traffic links, a park opposite, easy access to the West End and of course Wembley – Athena you can still pop along to Knightsbridge and Ares you can easily drive to the Emirates to watch the Gunners, and if we buy the adjoining properties we can ask the Three Fates and the Oracle at Delphi to move with us, though the 'Oracle at Neasden' doesn't have the same ring to it – maybe we should just simply call her 'The Sage'."

So, it came to pass that during the Olympian month of Skirophorion (which to us mortals equates to July), the Gods moved from Mount Olympus to their new modern home high on a hill in Northwest London, and although the postcode was NW2, it still gave them excellent views over the whole of London.

The British Government was generous in helping with

21

relocation as having the Olympians settling in the UK was a significant snub to the EU.

It goes without saying that as they were now officially residing in a North London postcode, they were able to get a Home Delivery Slot!

_____

First published on CaféLit 19 August 2020

The New Olympus Postcode: The Gods Find Work

Of course, the move to London wasn't that easy, and once the Gods of Olympus now officially known as the "Olympian Gods of North London" had settled in, they realised that they had lost their EU Major Deity Grants.

They now had to find work, as they were ineligible for state help, as their assets far exceeded the threshold for Universal Credit.

Zeus was invited by the Tory Government to become a Cabinet Adviser and teach them how to all develop a God Complex. His mode of dress, a gold trimmed Chiton, wide brimmed hat and a simple over the shoulder cloak, became an instant hit, and for many men became the favoured leisure wear, especially for those working in the city. The neatly trimmed beard, now universally adopted by the Millennials, a nod to the old days, completed the "Olympian Look".

Zeus was now officially a Special Adviser to the Government, or SpAd, but with his Olympian accent he always referred to himself as a Spud.

Apollo set up a discrete private medical practice in Harley Street that catered for the Healthy and Wealthy, and like many of the gods was approached by one of the Premiership clubs to join their board of directors. In direct contrast to his older brother Ares, Apollo together with his youngest brother Hermes, went for the Tottenham Hotspur option.

Tottenham's symbol of the cockerel whilst appealing to both gods (who were lords of both the Sun and Dawn), was hilarious, as it helped them both to constantly remind Ares – the God of the Red Planet Mars, and a strong supporter of their bitter rivals Arsenal – of his biggest faux-pas, when he was caught in flagrante with Aphrodite – his brother's wife.

Why? Because the bloody cockerel who was supposed to wake the couple at dawn fell asleep!

So to counter the chants of "Ares, Ares, he's one of our own, he's one of our own" from the Arsenal Fans; the Spurs boys came up with "na, na, na, na Apollo God of Men, God of Men, Apollo God of Men."

And for Hermes the Spurs faithful sang, "He's here, he's there, he's every f*cking where, Hermes, Hermes."

And as a final insult, whenever Arsenal came to the Spurs ground the Spurs supporters would all whistle the Rooster Song from the Robin Hood Cartoon, just to remind Ares of his past errors.

Ares himself hooked up with Nergal an old friend from Babylon nicknamed the "Boundary Stone" by his countrymen, and with both having now retired from being Gods of War, they set up a Security Consulting Service called "Styx and Stones Consulting".

Artemis and Athena opened a new boutique in Knightsbridge that sold clothes to the wives and girlfriends of the "Über Rich", continuing the theme they had started many years ago in Paris.

In contrast to the popularity of Zeus' Olympian look, their couture was based upon slim fitting single colour dresses, gold embroidered and precious jewelled tops, and exclusive skinny fit jeans, all made from natural and sustainable materials. All the clothing was individually hand sewn by a team led by Clotho (a member of the Three Fates), and Arachne "The Weaver".

Demeter who had previously spent most of her time in Hades, which had now relocated to the old, disused, closed, and very, very deep King William Street Underground Station. As she was now able to spend more time with her daughter, son-in-law, and grandchildren she got a job at the nearby Ministry of Ag, Fish and Food advising on cereal crops.

Hestia, alongside her Estate Agency opened an Olympus themed restaurant (on behalf of the other gods), called "Thalia", located in Belgravia, London. (www.olympiangods.com/thalia/bookings).

As would be expected Bacchus, as he now called himself, opened a microbrewery in Camden with help from his nymphs; and Aphrodite continued to stream her on-line "Adult Entertainment Channel". (www.goddessoflove@venus.com).

The Mechanic (Vulcan) remained in Cape Verde windsurfing.

Poseidon didn't move into the new residence with the others, preferring to house share with "Old Father Thames" in an abandoned fort in the Thames Estuary.

Hera stayed at home entertaining the great and the good, hosting a weekly book club, giving out prizes at the local schools, and working as a hospital volunteer. She also got a slot on London Radio hosting a weekly phone-in called *The Goddess Answers*.

So, the Olympian Gods of North London settled into their new home, fully integrating into the life and society of London; their new restaurant called "Thalia" in Belgravia soon became one of the go-to places in London.

First published on CaféLit 19 August 2020

The Loan

He knew his life was unravelling in an uncontrollable manner.

He was six months in arrears on his mortgage, massively overdrawn at the bank and had mounting gambling debts. He dared not stay away from the office, where he monitored the money transfers between the clients, dealers, and the firm, in case his office staff accessed his computer. He'd been siphoning money from the firm's accounts for the last few months to try and stem his personal financial haemorrhage. Now it was announced that in the next forty-eight hours the firm was bringing in external auditors to look for "financial irregularities".

He drove through the night picking up the A12 the other side of the Blackwall tunnel and headed north to Suffolk. During the drive he tried to calculate his total debt, which included how much he'd have to repay the firm if he didn't want to be on the opposite side of a jury in the near future. As the Mercedes purred northward, he figured that he needed ten million pounds to be comfortable but at a pinch he'd take seven and a half, and he hoped that the man he was travelling to see would help. He knew that once he was committed there was no wiggle room for negotiation or leaving the clutches of the MAN.

He crossed the Orwell keeping to the speed limit and entered East Anglia proper, turning off the A12 just north of Woodbridge. The houses were few and far between, mainly Georgian farmhouses or Victorian rectories, and as he neared his destination he slowed to a stop, and parking on the unlit roadside he lit up his second cigarette of the day, opened the windows and thought.

The man he was about to meet was how would he put it, rich, loaded, well off. Well, he had a lot of money, the result of drug and people smuggling, money laundering and arms dealing. He wasn't an easy man to deal with, dangerous to cross and never, ever, fail in your obligation if you've made a deal with him. He knew he was getting into bed with the Devil, but what could he do? He really had no alternative, but he had a proposal that he knew the MAN could not, would not overlook. He threw the finished cigarette out of the window and drove the remaining mile or so to his final destination and turning in he patiently waited for the electric gates to open and drove up the gravel drive to park in front of the large Georgian country house. He knew his entry was being monitored but still he was met by a youngish man, (armed he presumed), who silently led him through the large oak front door and opened the double doors to a large sitting room. He approached the distinguished looking silver-haired man sitting in front of the fire, who, looking up said, "Hello son. Good to see you."

He replied, "Hello Dad. I'm back and I need your help."

First published on CaféLit 19 November 2020

A Wrong Note

He stood watching in the corner of the square; the dawn was slowly breaking, and the hot moist night turned into an even hotter humid day. The mist rose lazily from the river obscuring his view of Algiers. The match flared as he lit yet another cigarette and silently and still, he watched and waited.

The heat became oppressive and sweat trickled down his back soaking through his crumpled linen shirt. In the heat, mosquitoes and fat flies buzzed around, but still he watched and waited.

The quiet of the early morning was broken by the sound of the first tram of the day as it clattered and clanged its way along the riverbank pausing at the far end of the square to disgorge it passengers. He could hear but not see the first ferry of the day lazily crossing the river to the island.

The hot sun continued to rise, bathing the old square in bright sunshine, and more people began to arrive, seeking shelter along its shaded edges and a few brave vendors began to set up their stalls in the square.

The match flared briefly; he took a long draw of yet another cigarette and in the heat of the day he silently watched.

The scream broke the silence and very soon he heard the wail of the sirens, and he knew that they had found his latest victim.

He felt no regret, no remorse, just sadness.

He remembered his time at the Conservatoire: the beauty of simple notes, of harmony, the strictness of the regime, the path towards the perfect chord. He'd tried to fulfil his quest as both pupil and teacher. Smiling to himself he ground out his cigarette and wiped the sweat from his forehead.

He turned on his heels slowly walking back out of the square to the roads behind, filled with clubs, absinthe and bourbon bars and restaurants. The music began to play, and he wandered from bar to bar, club to club, carefully listening to the notes played by the musicians blowing their saxes, cornets, and trumpets. He sat. He listened. He smoked. He sipped his bourbon, and then he heard it, a series of wrong notes. He stood silently, watched the musician responsible, and he knew in the heat of the day he had found his next victim.

First published on CaféLit 24 July 2020

The 12th Crusade – A Story of Another Time

In the year of our Lord 2024 Pope Urban IX and The Holy Roman Emperor, King Arthur VII of England called for a Western Crusade against China.

Since the beginning of the new millennium, "The Terrible Chinese Sickness" had swept the Americas and Western world four times with the loss of almost a third of the population.

The economies of the affected countries lay shattered and there was growing anger directed at the Chinese Empire where the sickness had begun its journey across the world.

The disease had been brought to Europe by ships and merchants travelling from the Far East to Europe, first landing in the big ports of Genoa, Marseille, and London.

The Church had first declared the plague, a punishment from God because of the pursuit of science and pleasure by the people of Europe.

In 2020 the church banned all science within the Holy Roman Empire and forbad its use by physicians in treating people affected by the plague, ordered that all Universities pursuing science be closed, and shut down all hospitals and medical schools not associated with the Church.

Belief in the Church became paramount and every wave of plague was greeted with the litany "God Wills It."

Before the sickness had arrived The Holy Roman Empire controlled and ruled almost half the world. At the outbreak of the "Pandemic", as the then Scientists had first called the "Terrible Chinese Sickness", the Holy Roman Empire itself had been a loose coalition of Empires and Kingdoms that had controlled and ruled not only the whole of Europe, but also the many Spanish, British and French colonies of the Americas as well as huge swathes of Afrika and India.

For over 500 years there had been relative peace in Europe, and the four powerful Empires of Britain, Spain, France and Germany had lived harmoniously alongside each other under the benign leadership of the elected Holy Roman Emperor and the Pope in Rome.

The current Holy Roman Emperor, King Arthur of England, was a direct descendant of Henry Tudor, or as British history always insisted on calling him, "Henry VII".

The descendants of Henry Tudor had over the many centuries, carefully and consistently ensured that the all those royal houses of Europe were closely interlinked by marriage, so that any transition of power was always smooth and untroubled, and always, always carefully guided by the Church in Rome.

Now in response to the call from Pope Urban IX and The Holy Roman Emperor, King Arthur VII of England together with his cousin, the eldest son of Louis XXII of France, were appointed by the Church to lead the combined armies of Europe against the Chinese Empire.

Included amongst this "Most Holy Army", as Rome was now calling it, were those armed forces of the English, Spanish, German and French empires together with their troops raised from their colonies in the Americas and Afrika.

The Russian Empire and the Russian Orthodox Church eagerly joined forces, and would now support, supply and reinforce this "Most Holy Army" in its crusade against China.

Commanding these massed forces were King Arthur's brother, Prince George Tudor; the Bishop of Mainz, Freidrich Hans Guderian, the notorious Russian Cleric Metropolitan Grigory Zhukov, and the French General Maximilian Bonaparte whose great-grandfather had conquered India for the French Empire.

At the Emperor's behest the Vatican lifted the 500year-old ban on muskets that had been ordained in the 7th Lateran Council of 1641.

As the crusading armies, now coming from all parts of Europe and their colonies in the Americas and Afrika, began to congregate in Western Russia. The Pope blessed the emperors, kings and commanders of the various armies in St. Peter's Square as they presented their Standards in preparation for the Crusade.

Amongst the banners raised, were the royal standards of England and Spain, the oriflame of France, the eagles of Germany, Russia and Poland, and the black cross of the Grand Master of the Teutonic Order.

Eastward the army would march, ever eastward to the far edges of the dark continent of Asia.

So, like a vast wave, the two million strong 12th Crusader army of Europe steadily moved across the vast plains of Russia and Kazakhstan towards China, much like their predecessors had done.

The army travelled not by foot or by horse, but by steam train and steam driven motorized vehicles, packed with men armed with the newest form of musket, crossbow, and artillery pieces, with the aim of laying waste to Wuhan and then onward to Peking. It would take months to move the army to the Chinese border where the enemy waited.

As the crusading army moved ever eastward, reports reached them of a Chinese army that had developed sinister weapons of destruction and a new form of transport that was translated as an "Infernal Combustion Engine" powered by a substance called Oyle. Weapons were said to be far more advanced than those of the Crusading Army, with a one being called a "rapid gun" capable of discharging hundreds of pieces of shot or "bullets" within a minute.

There were reports that the Chinese army had produced an evil machine called an "Armoured Fighting Vehicle" that carried a huge gun and armour to protect its men. Worse, being powered by Oyle, it could travel extremely fast.

Despite this King Arthur would gather his commanders and urged the armies ever onwards, repeating the mantra of the Church and Crusader, "God Wills it"; and so, the Crusader army of Europe moved slowly eastward to meet the Chinese army in the battle of Lake Balkash in Eastern Kazakhstan.

There was no Crusader miracle as there had been at Malta, Lepanto and Turkey, the battle was one sided and within seven days the crusading army of Europe was annihilated and the Chinese Empire moved Westward conquering all before them, completing what the "Terrible Chinese Sickness" had begun in the early days of the second millennium.

First published in *Aftermath*, Chapeltown Books, 2021

The Problem with Being a Superhero

The superhero looked at himself in the mirror. He looked good he thought: bulging muscles in all the right places, and sometimes in the wrong places, but nevertheless a credit to the superhero community. He wasn't an immortal, mutant or alien, nor was he imbued with any "Special Powers", just a normal fit and powerfully strong guy.

There were however a lot of things wrong with being a superhero, firstly the outfit. What idiot had deemed that superheroes had to wear their Y fronts outside of their tights? It wasn't a good look, and did it give you any additional support? Not on your life! He now had double hernias from all that leaping off tall buildings and lifting heavy objects. Oh yeah, it was OK for all those immortals and self-healing mutants but now he was contemplating surgery for his bilateral hernias and where would that leave him?

And the CAPE, the bloody cape, it was always getting caught in doors or snagged on bits of steel or whatever, and he had proposed getting rid of it.

"Oh no you can't," said the superhero community. "It's a de-rigueur fashion statement and marks us out as the good guys, lose it and you'll have to leave."

But the worst, the absolutely worst thing about being a Normal Human Superhero, was the bloody arthritis and joint pains he got from all the leaping about and fighting. His doctor had said that there was nothing he could do to stop the progress of the arthritic changes. Sure replacement joints may help, but that's more operations, months of pain and rehab and for what end? You can't replace the spine and your backache will only get worse. Try anti-inflammatories and painkillers and use a mobility scooter to get to the crime scenes!

So, this was the future he was now contemplating; it was one of joint pains and backache, wearing a support until he had his hernia surgery, wearing elasticated loose fit jogging bottoms, and travelling to the crime scene on his mobility scooter, and probably having to shoot the criminals to avoid a fight.

And *Oh Yeah* he'd still have to wear the bloody cape, billowing out behind at his now maximum speed of twelve miles per hour!

The Typewriter

The final demand from HMRC had arrived two days ago. In red the "request" had politely notified him that his unpaid tax bill had to be settled within twenty eight days or termination procedures would be enforced. No Ifs, No Buts, No Maybes, No Alternatives and certainly no "Payment Plan." Just a single sheet of paper with a single figure: pay or face "Termination Procedures".

On a bright note, if he submitted the final manuscript of his novel by the end of the week, he would receive the generous advance of £200,000 from his publisher, which should (or would) cover his tax bill and provide a bit extra that he could... Well... pay off some of his gambling debts... buy that new Porsche he wanted... pay off his various overdrafts?

He looked over to the old typewriter where he'd tried to write his novel. In the past it had served him faithfully: the clean sheets of paper, the sound of the keys, the movement of the carriage had all inspired him to write. This time nothing, absolutely bloody nothing entered his head: Rien, Nada, Nichts. He had tried writing in the conventional manner, pen (and pencil) on paper, he'd tried the cold sterile laptop, but nothing, nothing, had managed to motivate him as much as his grandfather's old typewriter, a throwback to the days of steam engines, petrol driven cars, and the wireless. Today's world of instant streaming, instant justice, instant payment (well to others anyway) and drone-based transport were all too urgent for his taste. All around were ripped, scrunched, and balled up pieces of paper, ashtrays full of cigarette butts, empty and half-drunk cups of coffee. He leaned back in the old leather armchair in the corner of his study, lit and took a long deep drag of the cigarette, and stared at the typewriter.

Fuck, one week to write a novel and pay the Revenue or

face what? If they didn't "Terminate" him then those bastards he owed money to would come after him, and what? Break his legs? Beat him to a pulp? Or yeah "Terminate him", and these were just the banks; he shuddered when he thought what those others he owed money to from his gambling, might do. Maybe "Termination" was a better option. No! No of course not, it would all be OK, wouldn't it?

He opened the window to clear the fug in his study. He sat down at the typewriter and inserted a fresh sheet of paper, and tried to write, he had to write. Damn! He stared at the typewriter, but nothing entered his head. He drank more coffee, smoked more cigarettes but nothing came. In anger and frustration, he picked up the typewriter and flung it out of the open window. Only then he remembered he wasn't at home, but in his London flat six stories up! Rushing to the window he watched the typewriter hurtle to the ground and watched as its descent was stopped when an Angel (well an airborne Police Patrolman with a flight backpack) swooped down and plucked it out of the air.

Open mouthed he watched as the Angel flew up, and appearing at the open window, flashed his warrant card and stated, "Sir, you need to be more careful; I'm issuing you with a summons to appear at the next Celestial Court," and drawing his pistol promptly shot him through the heart.

Some months later at an auction of his effects the bidding for his Vintage Olivetti Manual Typewriter started at £200,000.

———————

First published *Writes of Summer* 2017

The King's Troop

"The three thousand men of the King's troop stood firm as the enemy cavalry thundered toward them. In the centre stood a thousand lightly armed men in three lines, and either side were arrayed the archers. The bridge across the river anchored the left flank of the line heavily guarded so the enemy could not cross. On the right flank was the dense wood; through which mounted men could not pass. The king with his bodyguard stood dismounted in front of his men facing the enemy onslaught. The heavily armoured warhorses ridden by equally heavily armoured knights continued to charge, the earth shaking with their advance, yet still the King's men stood still. The dismounted warriors could see the steam rising off the warhorses and feel the thunder of the advance through their feet. At 300 yards the King's steward raised a red banner and 2000 archers unleashed hell. The arrows struck the beasts, the advance stumbled, broke and the charge was lost.

"And that Ladies and Gentlemen was how the young King won his first battle at this very bridge," said the guide.

The Final Hour

It was still dark; his watch showed four o'clock. He never could sleep the night before an operation. Around him his men were stirring, getting ready for the off which would start in an hour.

Absolute quiet were the orders from above, as was total secrecy.

He'd served with his men for the last three years ever since they'd marched into Russia; for three years they'd fought, advanced, and retreated through the cornfields of Ukraine and the Russian steppes, through the blazing hot summers and the cruel winters.

Here they were, back where they had started in 1940, grouped in the Ardennes ready to defend the borders of the Reich. To the South he could hear the rumble of artillery as the Americans tried to cross into the Saar, but here in the woods it was quiet, not even the sound of the allies' planes disturbing this moment of serenity.

This was madness.

"One last push, one last throw of the dice. Break the allies' spirit," they said. "Bring them to the table. A miracle would happen." Really?

Sure, the Yanks they were facing were raw recruits, recuperating GI's and thinly spread out; "Beak through, and get to Antwerp in three days," they ordered. Really?

Back when they had air support it had taken Uncle Heinz three days to cross the first river but then they had had Rommel leading the thrust, now he was gone, and Fat Hermann never delivered what he promised, so there were no planes and no support."

He remembered 1941: they had the best of everything men, tanks planes, and they rolled right over the Soviets. Now everything had changed, and Germany was fighting for its life, and what were the madmen in Berlin doing? Building "Super Weapons" which were never going to work and using the railways to transport Jews rather than men and supplies.

"We really, really, should have succeeded in July, but that's behind us and the only way is forward," he thought.

He looked at his watch: thirty minutes to go. Christmas was a few days away, and he wondered what the family was doing. Were they OK? Had they left Berlin? Were they in the country? His Estates in Eastern Prussia were too close to the Soviets, and he hoped to God they hadn't gone there.

He checked his watch: it showed one minute to five. OK. Time to go. Let's bring these "Allies" to the table and then deal with the real enemy, The Ivans.

The Baron, climbing up onto his tank, checked his watch, and at precisely 5 am the artillery barrage started; the panzers started their engines and slowly moved forward.

It was still dark; his watch showed four o'clock. The young US Colonel couldn't sleep and had driven forward to check on his men in their advanced positions.

Spread out thinly across the front, the men seemed in good spirits, truly believing the war would be over very soon. The enemy had all retreated back across the Rhine they said, the war will be over by Christmas they said, they'd all be going home very soon they said.

Standing up in his jeep looking through his binoculars he peered into the dark forest but could detect no movement.

The temperature continued to fall just like the winters back home in North Dakota, where his family, originally from Bavaria had settled in the 1860s. Now he was returning to the land of his ancestors at the head of a US Infantry Division.

What he wondered would his grandfather have thought of him? Old man Johan had been a Lawman in Bismarck in the latter years of the last century, and his father Heinz known as Harry had served with Pershing in France in 1918. Now it was his turn to bring law and order to this untamed land.

He checked his watch it showed five o'clock, time to return to his HQ. Suddenly the still dawn was shattered by the crashing sound of the artillery barrage and behind that the Colonel could hear the distinctive sounds of Panzer engines.

Years later the Baron would entertain the US Colonel on his Estate in Germany and the visit would always culminate in a driven shoot. When asked why they did this, the Baron remarked with a smile. "We spent years shooting at each other; now we do it together."

The Bus to the End of the World

The flyer dropped through his door early one morning. In bright red with bold white lettering it announced, "The Bus to the End of the World". Below the title it continued:

Transport for London is pleased to announce a new
    service from the weekend
Take the Bus to the end of the world,
See sights that'll amaze you,
Watch the changing stars,
Get to meet new and interesting people,
Take tea with the Old Gods,
Have cocktails with such celebrities as Bacchus, Thor,
    and Odin.
Eat Dinner in the Halls of Valhalla
Catch the bus at your nearest bus stop
Pre-Booking is recommended
All major credit cards accepted.
TfL permits the use of Oyster cards on this route
Concessionary travel cards will be honoured
Please book by going online at
    www.endoftheworld@elysium.co.uk

He quickly went online and found that there was a single slot left for that evening, so he booked it knowing that it was all free with his senior citizen bus pass.

So, what to wear for the event, he thought, opening his large wardrobe. He spotted a white blazer with vertical red stripes, perfectly complimented by white trousers, white shoes, and a white shirt. He topped this off with a red bowtie and a straw boater with a red-striped ribbon. Admiring himself in the mirror he thought, "I look just like Dick van Dyke in Mary Poppins!"

After a few minutes he muttered to himself, "That's

strange, I don't remember buying these clothes – oh well, they'll do."

Just after dusk he waited patiently alone at the bus stop, no one was around, and then he saw the bus; it was a new Routemaster. He remembered the old ones that he used to take to school when he was a boy in London. It was a number 937 – A prime number. The thought just popped into his head: *How did I know that?*

The destination shown on the front was, "The End of the World".

Getting on, he showed his bus pass to the silent driver and went upstairs to take a seat for a better view, but the windows were so dark he couldn't see out.

That was weird. There was no one else on board. Oh well, surely they'd pick up more passengers en-route.

After an indeterminate period of time during which he thought he must have dozed off and missed most of the journey, the Routemaster pulled up and the driver announced, "Last stop for the End of the World."

Looking around he realised he was the last one remaining on the bus. Strange. He hadn't seen any other passengers. He quickly descended the stairs and got off the bus. It was getting quite dark, and he initially thought he was alone.

Where were all the signs to the tearooms, restaurants, bars and Halls of Valhalla?

Out the corner of his eye he noted a number of black-clothed figures all heading toward some bright lights. He was intrigued to see that the lights flickered on and off and got brighter the closer he got to them.

Unexpectedly he was at a gate when a uniformed attendant shone a light in his face and asked, "Where is your admission ticket?"

"I, I don't have one." he replied, as the light grew brighter and more painful. "I didn't know I needed an admission ticket," he said, trying to turn away from the light. He found he couldn't, and it was now becoming increasingly more difficult to speak.

Suddenly he heard a voice. "It's OK, don't struggle. Welcome back Fred, you've been in a coma for the last month, but it's all-fine and you are back with us. There's a tube in your throat which is why you can't speak, so we're going to remove it now that you're awake."

First published on CaféLit 30 July 2020

Fleur's Story

At 41 Fleur knew time was running out. She was tired, very tired. She entered Kew Gardens by the North Entrance having crossed and re-crossed the bridge to make sure she wasn't being followed. She knew from the message drop she'd be meeting her handler by the Palm House.

She found a bench and sat. Reaching into her bag she took out her box of Sobranie Turkish cigarettes and placed one of the oval cigarettes between her ruby red lips and lit up. The sweet-scented smoke as always brought back memories. She'd been introduced to Turkish cigarettes by one of her many lovers during her time with the partisans in Yugoslavia.

Mikhail, she recalled, had been the local commander who met her when she was parachuted in by the SOE. She remembered his boyish good looks. She remembered his piercing blue eyes but most of all she remembered his body slumped on the ground after she had executed him: one shot Soviet style in the back of the head from the Nagant; the penalties of being an agent of the Abwehr. Mikhail had betrayed her. Andrei, a Soviet Communist, had rescued her from the Germans. Andrei made her whole again. Andrei had hunted down Mikhail and delivered him to Fleur for judgment.

For two years Fleur had fought alongside Andrei and his communist partisans as they liberated Serbia and Croatia pushing the German invaders progressively northwards.

It was the 1950s, England was a grey and tasteless nation, London was half bombed, and half rebuilt, but worst of all they (whoever they were) didn't want women or ex SOE mucking up their "Secret Service", preferring them as neat little secretaries in a boring 9-5 job.

Fleur had managed to get a job in the Foreign Office via her friends in the Ministry of Ag and Fish and the documents passing across her desk involved Foreign and NATO Policy towards various Eastern Bloc Countries and certainly were of interest to her handlers. She passed the information on, partly out of spite towards her country, partly in memory of her fallen Yugoslav comrades, but mostly for the money; her flat in Knightsbridge cost her an arm and someone else's leg as she used to joke to herself.

There was something familiar about the young well-dressed man that approached her but she couldn't quite put a finger on it. "Hello Fleur," he said. "We've not met but you're quite the hero to our people."

"My name is Peter Michaels," he continued looking directly at her with his piercing blue eyes, "and I'm attached to the Embassy; I'm here to take you to a safe place, where no-one will trouble you anymore."

With a sigh of relief Fleur replied, looking around, "I'm most grateful. I was worried that my past and present was catching up with me and there would be no future." Strange, the park was quiet and completely deserted.

"There is no future," he said as he shot her through the eye. Peter Michaels or "Petar Michailovich" as it stated on his embassy documents quickly strode away, satisfied that his father had been avenged.

———————————

First published on CaféLit 17 July 2020

The Hard Shoulder

Stranded on the hard shoulder at nine o'clock at night on a deserted motorway is one of the loneliest places on the planet. Moments earlier he'd suffered a rear blowout of his tyre.

Swerving across the three lanes of the road he'd managed to bring the car under control, and although it sounded awful, he'd coasted the car onto the hard shoulder, put on the hazards, and quickly got out of the car.

Shaking and with his pulse racing he tried to think what to do next.

Right, get the mobile phone, get the cigarettes, and get help in that order. The first two were on the nearside passenger seat so he retrieved them promptly and lit up a cigarette gradually calming his nerves.

Well, he'd survived so far. He convinced himself to look at the rear tyre. "Bloody hell" he said to no one in particular; the tyre was completely shredded, and the alloy wheel was sitting directly on the ground.

OK so what next? Who to call? For a start there was no spare tyre; the new Mercedes SL used run-flats only. "Pity they didn't prevent complete blowouts," he muttered to himself. So, he needed an emergency breakdown and recovery service but definitely not the police – stay behind the barrier for safety.

Bugger it. There was no service on his phone on this part of the deserted motorway. OK so where was the emergency telephone? There must be one either up ahead, or behind. He really didn't want the police involved.

Right. So get to the phone and call for an emergency recovery and get them to transport him and the car home; at least then he could sort this mess out.

There was little traffic around, but he really envied those driving past, snug, and warm in their heated cars, listening to the radio, they really didn't know how lucky they were.

He walked forward to the emergency phone, carefully keeping close to the barrier; he really didn't want to end up as another statistic of motorway fatalities.

There, about 200 yards ahead was one of the emergency phones, alone and isolated; it was an orange beacon, beckoning him closer. Once he'd picked up the handset he was quickly put through to an operator.

He quickly outlined his problem, emphasizing that the car was undriveable and requested an emergency recovery, agreed the price it was going to cost him and carefully detailed the make, model and registration of the car. He gave the operator the location number of the emergency phone making sure he stressed that the car was parked a few hundred yards behind the phone.

"I'm sorry, Sir, but could we have some credit card details for the emergency breakdown service," said the operator.

"No problem," he replied, pulling out the wallet from the pocket of his jeans, and reading out the long number, security code and expiry date, giving his name exactly as it was printed on the front of the card.

"Righto sir," replied the operator. "I'll have an emergency recovery truck with you in the next hour. Please return to the car but don't sit in it, and remain behind the barrier at all times."

He suddenly felt a lot calmer and thought it was all going to be OK.

He walked back to the car and was astounded to see two police cars parked slantwise behind the car with the police closing off the inner lane and diverting the traffic.

"Good evening, Sir." said one of the police officers. "Can we be of help?"

"No, no its OK, I've organised an emergency recovery

which will be here very soon. There's no need to worry. I'm perfectly safe and there's really no need for any fuss." He could hardly speak, as his mouth was now so very, very dry.

"Would you mind unlocking the car sir?" said a second policeman. "I'm sure everything is in order. We just need to see your insurance, and driving licence."

"They're all at home I'm afraid. I'll drop them into the nearest police station tomorrow, if that's OK," he replied.

"Could you step round to the boot sir?" demanded the first officer. As he opened the trunk, they all stared at the unconscious bound figure lying there. "Our very popular Assistant Chief Constable does love his new Mercedes, Sir."

First published on CaféLit 5 August 2020

The Particle

"Can you really travel back in time, without there being consequences?" asked Madam President.

The Pentagon, NASA and British Government had poured one hundred billion dollars into tachyon research in the hope of harnessing the particles that were thought to be capable of travelling faster than light. The British Government had been an eager partner and had made a significant contribution to the research programme, further enhancing the "Special Relationship" between the USA and United Kingdom.

Much of the research had been done in Antarctica, in the secure NASA Antarctic Transient Particle Unit. It was here that the NASA team had originally identified the tachyons, together with "High Energy" and "Sterile Neutrinos" as they were detected and captured by NASA's Antarctic Impulsive Transient Antenna. The researchers had first noted that these particles both appeared and disappeared instantaneously. Their mathematical calculations and modelling inferred that the particles were able to travel both backward and forward in time.

Over the last few years, their experimental studies had focused on studying whether the Tachyons and High Energy Neutrinos could possibly send firstly, labelled particles, and subsequently larger structures, and finally various organisms back in time. Now working under the umbrella of NASA, the US and UK researchers had all been uniformly successful, and today the 15th of April 2020, they were going to send the first live small animal backwards in time.

The auditorium in the Pentagon was packed with members of Congress, the Senate, Pentagon Officials plus a selection of British MPs and senior members of the UK

Armed Forces. Both Madam President and the UK Prime Minister were present, surrounded by their personal security teams and seated at the front. The images were going to be live-streamed directly from the isolated secure laboratory in Antarctica and the Director of NASA would be personally presenting the show in Washington.

"Madam President, Mister Prime Minister, Ladies and Gentlemen," the Director addressed the assembled audience, "we are about to witness the first transportation of a living animal backward in time using captured tachyons and high energy neutrinos. The images will be live streamed from the NASA Antarctic Transient Particle Unit. As the tachyons and high-energy neutrinos bombard the subject there will be some visual shimmering and the subject will disappear and reappear in exactly 3.84 seconds. This time lapse seems to be a constant which we've named the 'Malapero Constant'."

"Can you really travel back in time, without there being consequences?" asked the President.

"Yes, we can, Madam President" replied the NASA Director, "and today we hope to prove it. And there will be no consequences.

"OK, the team will answer any questions later, but we're about to start." He turned to face the large screen.

As the Director predicted, there was a shimmering effect on screen and the director thought that his vision blurred for an instant and as anticipated, the subject disappeared and reappeared in exactly 3.84 seconds.

As the Director turned around to the assembled audience, the US President stood up, and said, "Wonderful, wonderful, very, very exciting, I always said it would work, 'World Beating Tachyon Technology!' " He was still wearing his trademark red baseball cap…

The Dusk Walkers

Did you notice sometimes out of the corner of your eye, sometimes in the shadows, the number of people who were out in the early hours of the morning, usually alone very occasionally in pairs? They kept to the shadows, silent and watching. Both men and women any age, all with bright shining eyes. If you approach them, they'll quickly and silently walk away, their only distinguishing feature being their eyes. Who are they? What are they watching? What do they want? And what do they do?

It all began during the virus lockdown in 2020. I had returned to help out at the local hospital where I'd worked as a surgeon for the previous twenty-five years. Although retired I responded to the request for retirees to volunteer to help out. My role was simple: it was to check on patients who'd been discharged from hospital or those who'd reported mild symptoms of the viral disease to their GPs. After contacting many patients, I became aware that some were reporting severe symptoms of recurrent persistent eye pain and a hypersensitivity to light, or as we medics like to call it, photophobia. I duly filled in the contact forms highlighting the symptoms described but during the height of the epidemic everyone was far too busy to comment.

After working in the hospital for about a month I tested positive for the virus but had no symptoms. However, a couple of weeks later I started to experience severe eye pain, and sensitivity to light. The pain was so severe I couldn't sleep but wasn't tired despite preferring the night hours to sit outside in the garden, doing little more than listen to audiobooks or the news.

Over the next few weeks, the pain became less but the light sensitivity remained. Interestingly my night vision improved so much that it seemed on many an occasion night became day. I found it difficult to go out in the bright daylight without sunglasses and my vision became clearer and crisper so much so that I had to discard my glasses that I always wore full time. The only problem was that I seemed to have a number of floaters in both my eyes.

As lockdown was eased, I managed to get an appointment at my optician's who confirmed that my vision was now perfect, the short-sightedness and severe astigmatism had completely reversed, but he was troubled by the changes in the eye about which he jokingly stated, "If I didn't know better I'd say that you've got gold flakes in your eyes, which is why they look bright and shiny – I've never seen that before! Look I'll arrange for you to see one of the guys at Moorfields Eye Hospital. I'm sure there's nothing to worry about. At least you don't have to buy any glasses!"

At Moorfields the consultant was puzzled and called in one of his colleagues to have a look, then another, and another and finally the professor was asked to have a look. Nobody came up with an answer, so I was asked to stay in "for a number of tests" as they put it.

I was given a nice private room and was subjected to scans, bloods, numerous eye examinations, and visits by several ophthalmic surgeons, neurologists and a couple of doctors who introduced themselves as metabolic specialists.

I must have given a pint and a half of blood and the conclusion at the end of this? Yup: I had deposits of gold flakes in my eyes – why? It must be a consequence of the virus infection they said – how? Well, here's the outline as I can remember. There's a series of enzymes in the body classified as Cytochrome P450 that has a huge range of functions which include binding heavy metals to form what's called a metallo-enzyme. We all have a bit of gold in our bodies notably around the heart, in the joints and in our nerves. Somehow the viral infection subtly altered the function of the Cytochrome P450, which allowed it to leach out the gold from its normal sites, and for some reason deposited it in the eyes.

Jokingly they said that maybe this was the basis of the Goose that laid the Golden Egg story? Really! So, what next? I asked. Well – pause – we don't really know, but yours is not the first. We've now heard of many similar cases throughout the country and from Europe. Someone has even coined the name "Goldeneye Syndrome". What next – we don't know, but it would seem that the condition should, emphasizing the SHOULD, stabilize, as there is only a small amount of gold in the body that can be deposited. Stay out of the sun, wear sunglasses, eat a healthy diet, and we'll keep a regular and close eye on you.

So it was, the days turned into weeks, I avoided the daylight hours and lived my life in the dusk and night and on occasion I would meet someone in the shadows with the same problem. You could identify us by the fact that we wear sunglasses at night or by our shining metallic eyes. It was all going OK till the news broke on TV with the exclusive, titled *They Carry a Fortune in Their Eyes*.

Now I hear that people with Goldeneye, or even anyone wearing sunglasses are being hunted for their eyes, and I can't go out anymore.

There are no more Dusk Walkers around.

Where have they all gone?

Where can I go?

First published on CaféLit 8 August 2020

Reductio ad Absurdum

It seemed like everywhere I looked I saw Angels.

Well, they weren't really angels; it was the name we gave them. Their ship had crash-landed thirty-five years ago in the relatively deserted Suffolk countryside, and the crew of twenty-five aliens had grown in number to around 100. The aliens, who were peaceful in nature, were essentially humanoid in appearance; all had long white hair and deep black eyes. Their distinguishing feature were the two large wings emerging from their backs, which is why they were nicknamed "Angels".

It transpired that the wings were part of their respiratory system providing a membrane that allowed oxygen to directly access their bloodstream, an evolutionary response to their world, whose oxygen levels had progressively fallen over the many millennia of their existence.

Despite their many issues they were a happy race, always singing and dancing – oh how they loved to dance! Despite this the Angels had an astute scientific mind and were able to understand complex mechanical problems, and combined with their scientific and astrophysics knowledge were able to adapt at least for a while, to their time here on Earth.

The alien ship, beautifully designed, looking like an extended fattened needle with a flattened base, had been one of many launched from their home world to search for suitable planets for colonization. The alien community had been happy to share their technology with our world, especially the workings of their proton impulse engine, which had allowed them to cross the vast distances of space. The payment was simple: we had to help repair their needle-ship and allow them to depart to try and return to their home. It had taken thirty-five years and the combined efforts of many of the world's leading scientists helped by their Angel counterparts to carry out effective repairs on their needle-ship, which had been nicknamed THE PIN, because of both its appearance and its proton impulse needle drive.

My role as Senior Scientific Adviser to the British Government was to inform the Angel Community that their ship was now ready, and to supervise their departure.

Some months later, as the Angels danced, skipped and made their way onto their ship, I looked around the Angel community and idly wondered, "How many Angels can dance in the hold of a PIN?"

NOTE

Reductio ad Absurdum (reduction to absurdity), is a form of argument that attempts to establish a claim by showing that the opposite scenario would lead to absurdity or contradiction. The best example is the discussion surrounding the question *"**How many angels can dance on the head of a pin?**"* The debate is most commonly linked to the fall of Constantinople, with the image of scholars debating whilst the city was being besieged; essentially it is a metaphor for wasting time debating topics of no practical value, or questions whose answers hold no intellectual consequence, while more urgent concerns accumulate.

First published on CaféLit 17 October 2020

Retiral

It was the last week in his job. He was old, well fifty-five was old for his current employment, he'd served a long apprenticeship and for the last twenty-five years he'd worked for the same employers. They'd been very generous in their pay, support and had provided many all-expenses paid vacations.

He'd been loyal to his employers, courteously refusing other job offers and had turned down freelance work unless his employers had agreed.

Over the years he'd lived a charmed life, and was lucky that he enjoyed his work. How many people could say that?

Together with his employers he'd set up a training program that throughout the community he worked in was acknowledged as being the best there was, and despite the pressures of their profession his trainees had gone on to practice their trade throughout the world.

His employers had acknowledged that the time was now right for him to retire and ensured that he would receive a generous pension package and had even appointed a successor to his position, a young lad that he'd fully trained in the art, skill, and ethos of their profession, but they had politely requested that he stay on to complete one last assignment.

Still fully fit and in his prime he'd happily agreed and had packed his bag and the tools of his trade and had taken the company's private jet to London.

So here he was, in one of the best cities in the world, looking forward to a long retirement and about to complete his last assignment for his employers.

He carefully adjusted the Sig Sauer Sniperscope to focus on his selected target and gently squeezed the trigger.

He saw the target fall to the ground.

He'd now successfully completed his last sanctioned assignment and was now officially retired.

The Eye

The last time the eye had blinked was thirty-five years ago.

The first time he'd studied the Helix Nebula or NGC7293, as it was officially classified, was when he was a twenty-five year old grad student working on his PhD thesis titled *Spectroscopic Analysis of the Expansion Rate of the Outer Rings of NGC7293*. In simple terms he was analysing the growth rate of the Nebula.

He'd continued to study and photograph the Nebula every day (well almost), for the last thirty-five years.

What made it so special? Simply put, the Nebula looked like an eye and had been nicknamed by the media as "The Eye of God" or "The Eye of Sauron" but the names were simply that, a nickname.

In truth, as he always stated, "The Helix Nebula was just a simple planetary nebula with a dying star at its core. The hot dense core giving off intense radiation was thought to be responsible the appearance of the nebula as an eye."

Thirty-five years ago, as a young grad student he'd been convinced that the eye had blinked, but did he tell anybody or publish it, "not on your life!" He'd have been subjected to ridicule, his career terminated, and PhD binned.

Nevertheless, his fascination with the Nebula had remained and he continued to monitor and study the "Eye" as he called it, throughout his academic life.

Now as professor of astrophysics at one of the most reputable universities in the US, he had his own team of students that continued to study, measure, and monitor the Nebula.

The department had access to not just the Hubble and newer James Webb telescopes, but also NASA's Spitzer Space telescope for infra-red analysis, the Galaxy

Evolution Explorer for ultraviolet emissions and a whole array of spectroscopic and radio telescopes.

His team excitedly reported that the eye had appeared to blink – "No, there was no evidence of cosmic dust" – "No, there was no apparent change in temperature differentials" – "No, the central core had not imploded, or exploded," and as they all chorused "there were no changes in the spectroscopic analysis."

Infrared photography clearly showed that the Helix Nebula had blinked.

Other Astrophysics departments began to confirm the team's findings, surely there was a scientific explanation for this, or was this just an astronomical anomaly?

As the sudden massive burst of solar radiation burnt out all the electronics on Earth he wondered, truly, did the Eye of God really blink?

Now he would never know.

First published on CaféLit 15 August 2020

The Object

They first tracked the extra-terrestrial object when it was thirty-five million miles out from Earth. Contrary to expected observations its rate of acceleration appeared to slow, and its projected path would take it very near to Earth, about twelve million miles out, in astronomical terms a close flyby, and it was now classified by NASA as a "Near Earth Object".

As it slowed the object appeared to emit a repetitive Fast Radio Burst lasting two milliseconds and repeated every two hours for two days then went silent only to recur at eight -day intervals.

Until that point the object had been classified as a comet, but the pattern of acceleration, the fast radio bursts and the projected course ruled out it being any form of cometary body, but its origin was most clearly from outside of the solar system.

The teams at Cornell and McGill Universities both confirmed that the radio burst from the object exactly matched a signal they'd been tracking for the last fifteen years. The team at Cornell had backtracked the signal to a group of stars in the Auriga constellation in the northern spiral arm of the Milky Way.

At a meeting of NASA's Near-Earth Object Observation Team, it was confirmed that the object was on a trajectory that would swing it past Earth and subsequently leave the Solar System twenty degrees above the orbital plane, as the object passed through the orbits of Mars and Saturn it would head out in the direction of the Auriga constellation.

Both the NASA and the European Telescopes in Hawaii and Chile confirmed that the object was cylindrical in shape, approximately half a kilometre in length, with no visible propulsion systems but spun along its long axis every eight hours.

Over the next three months the observatory teams confirmed that as it passed its the nearest point to Earth (the perigee), it had now begun to accelerate out of the Solar System despite the gravitational pull of the Sun and the other planets.

Throughout this time the fast radio bursts had continued, but by day 120 after reaching its perigee, and with the object now accelerating rate of departure, they suddenly ceased.

Calculations by the Near-Earth Object Team showed it would leave the Solar System by year ten after its closest approach to Earth if it continued at its current rate of acceleration.

The questions the NASA Team asked were how was it accelerating?

Where did it originate?

Where was it headed?

Both MIT in Massachusetts and Caltech in Pasadena proposed a light or magnetic sail as a possible means of obtaining thrust.

As for its origin, that would be unknown, but the preliminary orbital calculations showed that it came from the approximate direction of the bright star Capella (or alpha Auriga) in the constellation Auriga.

A probable orbital plot adjusting for changes in stellar positions concluded that the orbit of the object might have previously bypassed Earth some sixty-five million years earlier. The NASA team now named the object "Kaitiro" (the Observer).

A palaeontologist at Caltech later pointed out that if it had travelled near Earth some sixty-five million years earlier, then it would have coincided with the last Mass Extinction Event…

First published on CaféLit 25 August 2020

The Lone Bomber

The American built B17 Flying Fortress was alone in the dark sky above France as it flew in a south-western direction, Strasbourg was now far behind them, they'd dropped their payload a couple of hours earlier.

The four-engine plane had been fully rebuilt after a crash landing some months earlier, following an Allied bombing raid on Hanover. Now fully operational and crewed by its full complement of ten men, it steadily flew on; the US built Pratt and Whitney engines working harmoniously.

For the ten-man crew it had been a long, long, war and by late summer 1944 they were exhausted; they'd flown numerous missions into and out of Germany and France, and somehow, they'd all survived.

Below them were the flashes of artillery fire as the Allies continued their advance across Northern France but the Lone Bomber continued in its south-westerly route hoping to avoid any anti-aircraft fire.

Unexpectedly, below, and ahead of them they saw a formation of American B17s obviously heading home and their plane joined the rear of the flight, giving their call sign of the 392nd Bomber Group.

Switching radio frequency, the wireless operator, a farmer's son from North Dakota, confirmed that they'd been separated from their group somewhere over Stuttgart. The flight they joined acknowledged their presence and the Flight Commander in his Bostonian accent welcomed them to temporary membership of the 41st Bomber Group "Party", and happy to provide them with company and an escort home.

Over Clermont-Ferrand they ran into unexpected heavy anti-aircraft fire and were pounced on by a pack of German

Fighters. The flight of B17s broke up, and to escape the ground fire and fighters the bomber turned due south and was soon over Toulouse.

The Lone Bomber continued in its southerly route, crossing the Pyrenees into Neutral Spain. It had clearly taken a hit as one of the engines now failed, but with three engines running and adequate fuel, the navigator calculated they could reach Valencia on the Mediterranean coast of Spain.

As the B17 rolled to a stop in the early dawn on the runway at Manises Airport just to the west of the city of Valencia, its *Luftwaffe* markings could be clearly seen, with the *Hakenkreuz* or swastika emblazoned on its tailfin. The ten-man crew climbed down from the aircraft and drank in the fresh morning air of Spain.

The German Luftwaffe Special Forces men of *Kampfgeschwader 200* had finally left the war far, far behind, and the four agents they had dropped over Northern France would have to fend for themselves. The war was lost anyway, so why worry?

First published on CaféLit 9 September 2020

Two Crocs on the Beach

We sat together on the beach, watching the waves breaking. The wind whipped up and the waves grew higher and crashed with increasing ferocity. A couple of brave surfers appeared in front of us, clipped on their boards to their ankle harness, left their shoes on the pebbled beach and strode out into the sea.

We continued to watch as they lay on their boards and half paddled half swam out into the waves.

Far out they waited on their boards and successfully rode the waves into the shore. The waves got higher and faster, and the surfers continued to ride their boards. It was impressive but to us it seemed foolhardy. The skies darkened the wind increased and we decided to leave the beach for shelter and food. Walking off the beach we noticed that one of the surfers had weighed down his green crocs with stones to prevent them being blown away. As we passed his shoes one of the surfers had clearly given up and rode up on the shore and unclipped his board, put on his shoes and like us walked off the beach. The other, presumably the owner of the green crocs, remained out on his board far out to sea. We could just make out his head bobbing in the water.

We returned to the beach a couple of hours later. The surfer was nowhere to be seen but his shoes were still on the beach.

The following morning we again returned to the beach and the green crocs were still there, still weighed down by their stones. Had the surfer forgotten them, had he drifted down shore, or had he been washed out to sea? We didn't disturb the abandoned shoes. I did inform the local coastguard, but nothing was ever reported back, nor were there any stories about a missing surfer in the local news.

Over the years I've often wondered what happened to the owner of the green crocs.

_____

First published on CaféLit 7 October 2020

Quick in, Quick out

The house was dark; no lights showed. It was one of those "between the wars" detached houses that can be seen all over London. He knew that the elderly couple that lived there were alone, and as it was two O'clock in the morning were unlikely to be awake. There was no obvious alarm system and he pushed open the side gate and very quietly tried the back door to the kitchen which he surprisingly found unlocked, pushed open the door and entered the property.

He'd done this many times before and would continue to do so. Burglary was in his blood; it was all he knew. He never robbed multiple properties in the same street; "just the once", he liked to think. London was large enough for him to work every night without revisiting the same street. Of course, it got harder with more alarm systems being installed, but he knew that the older the occupant the less likely a fitted alarm, but a higher likelihood of a better haul. He avoided electronics, concentrating on jewellery, cash, small pieces of art, only stuff he could put into the bag he had slung over his shoulder.

There were no sounds in the house; he spotted a small figurine on the hall table, which he placed in his bag. He quietly climbed the stairs and pushed open the door to the first bedroom. No sounds but there were clearly two people in the bed: no movement, no sound. He crossed the room to the bed and shone his light onto the elderly couple who were clearly asleep, or were they dead? No sound, no movement, and no breath sounds. He touched the forehead of the old man, still slightly warm. He put his ear against the old man's mouth, no breaths. The old man had a big gold signet ring, which he removed. He repeated the process with the other occupant, and removed her rings, the diamond pendant still around her neck, and leisurely removed other items of jewellery from the bedroom. He cast one backward glance before he closed the door, quickly descended the stairs, and left the house. *Quick in, quick out,* he thought, as he briskly walked away. Thankfully with lockdown due to the virus there were very few people and cars about, certainly no police.

When he arrived home, he hid the night's collection, with the others from his six previous robberies.

He would have to cash in when lockdown was over, he thought, as he tried to suppress his cough.

Ten days later the Intensive Care Unit Nurse switched off his life support. "Pity," she said behind her protective mask and visor. "I thought we could save this one."

Valentine's Day

In the summer of 1816 Valentine Day, the third son of the Earl of Luxborough, left England for the Americas. As a third son, he had no prospects, no money and as they would often say "no expectations". He had managed to sell his commission and the money gained helped to pay for his passage to Boston.

He had plied his trade as a soldier in the British army for fifteen years firstly in South America and following the defeat at Montevideo had followed Black Bob Craufurd back to England and had joined the Fifty-Second Foot for the duration of the Spanish campaign, and then followed Wellington to the Low Countries.

He'd fought in line against the French column, in square against their cavalry; he'd fought with musket and bayonet on the ground, with sabre on horseback. He'd fought in the mountains of Portugal, the plains of Spain, and the fields of France. He'd fought under the blazing sun and in the torrential rain, he had marched from Lisbon to Porto, and he had marched across Spain and into France.

The Victory of 1815 had left little prospects for an Infantry Captain in peacetime. He was not wanted back home at the family estate, and London was full of discharged officers looking for work.

Over the next two years Valentine travelled from Boston to St. Louis finding work on cotton and tobacco plantations, building the new canals heading west, and hunting buffalo on the plains.

His travels took him across Virginia, Kentucky, Tennessee and finally into the Mississippi Territory and St. Louis.

The old trading post had been acquired in the Louisiana Purchase some years earlier, and now was a bustling city with banks springing up alongside brothels, saloons, and fur trading houses. Across the river was the vast Missouri Territory unmapped and ripe for the taking.

Valentine crossed the Mississippi in the summer of 1818 armed with his old Baker rifle, powder and shot, plus two horses and four mules, with the aim of carving out some land to grow either cotton or tobacco. The warning about the danger of the Creek Indians and their more violent brothers the Red Sticks was ringing in his ears as he headed west.

Ten days after crossing the river, Valentine chanced upon an encampment of the Muskogee, he entered the settlement signalling that he came in peace and noticed a Creek woman of intense beauty when cupid's arrow struck.

But it wasn't; it was the white-feathered arrow from the bow of a Red Stick Brave.

So Ended Valentine Day – Honourable Soldier and failed Explorer.

The Trouble with Chicken

As he drove on the I-985 towards Atlanta he thought how his road trip to New Orleans had been delayed by a couple of days and he started humming his own version of *I Fought the Law and I Won.*

It had all started simply with him having left New York far behind four days ago. The plan was to drive his car down from New York to his new home in the Warehouse district in the "Big Easy".

The old 911 had purred along nicely and he'd taken his time on the trip, discovering parts of the US he'd be unlikely to ever visit. He was not due to start his new job as a professor in surgery at the University Medical Centre, for another month, so time was not pressing.

He'd arrived in Gainesville, Georgia, intending to stop over for a couple of days, hire a boat and do a day's sailing on nearby Lake Lanier, before heading further south.

He'd booked a couple of nights at the Hampton Inn and had wandered along to the concierge's recommendation of the "Best Chicken Inn in Town".

Over fifty years ago Gainesville had proudly proclaimed itself the "Poultry Capital of The World" and this particular restaurant was claimed to be the best in town. He'd ordered the House Special and a selection of sides and picking up his knife and fork he settled down to eat his huge plateful of fried chicken.

He'd have eaten his meal with relish, but as he'd finished his plate of fried chicken, he noticed that the restaurant had gone quiet and standing opposite him was a tall deputy sheriff wearing mirrored sunglasses who looking at him said, "Sir, please stand up and turn around, I'm arresting you for violation of the City Ordinance of the 15th of January 1961."

Speechless, he'd meekly obeyed and felt the handcuffs being applied. All he could think was that he'd violated some local traffic ordinance, and this could be easily dealt with.

He'd been taken to Hall County Jail, where he'd been photographed, processed, and placed in a cell by himself. The deputy sheriff informed him that he'd be appearing before the judge the next day when a trial date would be set, and if he wished, a court appointed attorney would be made available. He'd been allowed to call his brother who was an attorney in Manhattan, and he'd agreed to fly down first thing, in time for his court appearance.

The following afternoon he'd appeared before the judge, when his brother had argued that his arrest had violated his First Amendment Rights, which included the "Freedom of Expression." As expected, the case was dismissed, and he'd been allowed to go free.

His brother disappointedly stated, that he wished the case had gone further, as he'd love to have taken it all the way to the Supreme Court.

After all a City Ordinance dating from 15th January 1961 which made it "illegal to eat fried chicken in Gainesville with a knife and fork" really should be repealed.

———————

First published on CaféLit 26 October 2020

The Return Flight

The flight to Lisbon took off on time, there were no bomb craters to negotiate and Bristol had not suffered a night bombing for the last week. The twice-weekly flight from Whitchurch to Lisbon was operated by BOAC, running a number of KLM owned Douglas DC-3's. The flight time with a maximum of twenty-two passengers was just over five hours and was always full.

Colonel Charles Henderson of the Foreign Office looked around; it was not his first flight and would certainly not be his last. Henderson was a member of the War Office Military Intelligence Directorate, dealing with German Intelligence, and the Colonel was flying out to Lisbon on behalf of the War Office to meet a representative of the German High Command.

His briefcase carried a variety of documents, which, if they fell into the wrong hands, would be of little consequence; what was more important was the single sheet stitched into the lining of his jacket.

As he looked around, the colonel noted that the passengers on the plane included mainly businessmen, a couple of uniformed British Army officers, and three Free French officers, who were presumably going to pick up the BOAC Flying Boat to Bathurst in The Gambia, West Africa to meet with Vichy officers of the French West Africa Forces.

It was November 1943; the war in Russia and the East had clearly turned in the Soviet's favour following the surrender at Stalingrad, the huge German failure at Kursk, and the Russian entry into the Ukraine.

The appearance of US forces into Europe had permitted the invasion of North Africa, Sicily, and Italy to take place. British and US bombers were now carrying out constant daily raids over Germany. There was no doubt that German defeat was inevitable, though how long that would take, was anybody's guess.

Neutral Lisbon had become a hotbed of intrigue, the centre for the exchange of intelligence, and the organisation of international business deals. Both Allies and Axis nations maintained full embassy staff in addition to the numerous spies and agents that had gravitated to the city.

The man Henderson was going to meet was a high-ranking staff officer attached to Wilhelm Keitel's staff in the German Armed Forces High Command.

In an effort to save the four million men of the German army in Russia from complete destruction, General Keitel, the Head of the German Armed Forces had made a circuitous approach to the British Ambassador in Buenos Aires in late September 1943, seeking talks with the British Government regarding the complete surrender of all Axis Forces to the Allies. Additionally, Keitel had offered to travel to Great Britain via Lisbon to negotiate the cessation of hostilities. Henderson was carrying the official reply from the British Government regarding further negotiations.

His message duly delivered and with an overnight stay in Lisbon under his belt, Henderson was now returning to Bristol on BOAC flight 777 accompanied by a senior military attaché from the British Embassy in Lisbon.

Before he had taken off, Henderson had witnessed the departure of the Deutsch Lufthansa Junkers Ju-52 carrying the German staff officer returning to Berlin conveying the official British government's response.

It was possible, just possible that this could result in an early end to this awful war.

BOAC Flight 777 had departed Portela Airport in Lisbon on schedule some two hours following the departure of the German plane, and take off was smooth. As with the outward-bound journey, the flight was full, and carried a number of civilians, army officers and diplomatic staff.

The DC-3 flew steadily northwards crossing the northern Spanish coast into the Bay of Biscay when Henderson observed that their plane was being accompanied by a flight of six Luftwaffe Ju-88s.

"I hope they're simply an escort and not a threat," said Henderson to his embassy colleague.

"A curious maritime patrol I suspect; despite the conflict we have an agreement on allowing these civilian flights to proceed unmolested," replied the diplomat. "I really hope we're undisturbed, as this could be the one last chance of peace between our countries before the Eastern front turns into a greater killing field than it already is."

But it was too late. The DC-3 shuddered from the cannon fire from the Luftwaffe fighters and began its final fatal dive into the grey seas of the Bay of Biscay.

The flight commander or Staffelführer, a Colonel in Luftwaffe Kampfgeschwader 40, had received direct orders from Reichsmarschall Hermann Göring himself, to seek out and destroy BOAC flight 777 once it had left Portuguese airspace and was out over the sea, with the words "Surrender is not an option".

First published on CaféLit 3 November 2020

The Leaping Tiger

The foreign volunteers of the 950th Infantry Regiment had been rapidly retreating backwards from Bordeaux across France towards the Alsace-German border. Harried by Allied soldiers and French Resistance fighters the regiment suffered increasing casualties as they fought back with their usual tenacity.

It was not for nothing that the regiment was considered one of the more elite units within the German army, clearly recognised by its distinctive badge of a "Leaping Golden Tiger".

The men had spent the preceding six months based around the beaches of Bordeaux, resting training, and refitting in relative peace. They had welcomed their numerous reinforcements – more of their countrymen, who immediately felt comfortable amongst their comrades, despite the majority of their commanding officers being German.

Their unit culture represented a home away from home; they cooked and ate their own food, practised their own religion, and despite the necessity of wearing the field-grey of the German Army they were free to select their own national and religious headdress.

The allied invasion in June and its subsequent drive south meant that the battalion had to pull out of the relative serenity of Bordeaux and head backwards to join the gathering German forces who were preparing to defend the very borders of the Fatherland, though not their Fatherland. Like the many other foreign battalions and divisions they would fight to protect their adopted masters – after all where else could they go? Home was far, far away, and would they be welcomed back? Possibly, possibly not, but considering the political upheaval at home, that welcome would be sometime in the future.

They made a stand against the Allied forces outside of Dijon, but their defence failed in the face of the overwhelming superiority in allied numbers; and they continued to flee northward, pursued on the ground by US troops, and constantly harried from the air by Allied planes.

The remaining survivors of the regiment attempted to regroup alongside other German units to face the advancing allies, who proved far too strong. The remnants of the regiment continued their retreat, finally crossing the Rhine into the safe refuge of their adopted Fatherland.

Those surviving members finally encamped outside of the town of Stetten just a few kilometres north of Lake Constance, and very close to the Swiss border to refit and re-arm in preparation for their final defence.

It was here that it was announced that they, like all other Foreign Volunteer Regiments had been subsumed into Himmler's *Waffen-SS,* but the men of the regiment had little idea as to the implications of this re-designation. All they knew was that they were now renamed as a *Volunteer Legion of the Waffen-SS.*

Now in the South of Germany, in relative isolation, they received news of the entry of Allied troops into the Fatherland, and the progressive collapse of their adopted country.

Fearing for their future the remaining men of the "Volunteer Legion" marched the short distance to the German-Swiss Border to seek sanctuary in Switzerland, but the Swiss ever mindful of their neutrality would not allow them entry.

The men of the Legion had little option but to surrender to the US Army in the hope that, by avoiding capitulation to the British, they would not be tried and executed for treason.

Those surviving one thousand men of the *Free Indian*

Legion of the Waffen-SS had deserted the British Indian Army and had fought against their ruler and emperor: the British Raj.

First published on CaféLit 22 November 2020

The Diary of a Millennial Vampire

Thankfully I settled back into the first-class seat. I had a feeling of euphoria; soon very soon the "Hunger" would disappear, and I'd be able to enjoy some food for the first time in eighteen months. Well, at least the "Hunger" would not return until the flight landed in Buenos Aires in sixteen hours or so.

I don't suppose you've given it any thought, but the Covid 19 pandemic has been particularly bad for us in the vampire community. What with the restrictions on movement, especially at night, and until the advent of the immunization programme, you couldn't just bite anybody. I mean we're all mostly immune to blood borne diseases, but not to the Covid virus, which seemed to have had a particularly bad effect on our community.

We all know, that as supposedly creatures of the night, we lack vitamin D which made us all increasingly susceptible to the effects of the virus – go on, read all the newspaper reports on vitamin D deficiency and susceptibility to the Covid virus.

Then when "Lockdown" came, we couldn't just go and knock on doors and be invited over the occupier's threshold. And just to let you know, we don't use violence or a gun to force entry, just good old animal magnetism – it gets us in every time. It all went downhill from there; you can't get a "click and collect" or a "home delivery" for a pint of fresh blood.

So there we were, isolated, stuck at home, and worse off all, unable to go out and feed. We're not immortal or unkillable just long-lived – well for a few centuries or so, but we do need a regular supply of fresh blood to satisfy our "Hunger". Sure, you can get by on stored blood, but its long-term use is not recommended, it clearly states that in the *Handbook of Vampyr Well Being*.

On top of that, the streets were empty; there was nobody

around – remember? The only people you were likely to encounter were others from our own community, and that really, really doesn't work for us at all.

The only members of the vampire community, who were less troubled, were those who lived-in high-rise flats, but they needed to be above ten floors or higher. For some reason the higher you go off the ground the less "The Hunger" troubles you. I mean there's no logical reason for it. It just is - and living up a mountain doesn't help; you must be physically off the ground.

I really don't know why in all the old vampire films, we're portrayed as living underground, even in coffins! That's so wrong. I hate cellars and coffins and the fact that living a high-rise life diminishes "The Hunger" is a somewhat recently observed phenomenon – well, ever since our American cousins started building so-called skyscrapers.

Then in the 1940s one of our brethren had a light bulb moment – that's OK – light bulbs are fine, but as in all the folklore, it's the sunlight that causes the problem, not artificial lighting. I mean who doesn't like going out in the evening for a drink, a meal or even clubbing? I may be old but I haven't aged for a couple of hundred years and can still mix it with those modern Millennials.

Sorry I digress; it's the euphoria of freedom, the flight and the temporary easing of "The Hunger".

Anyway, in the 1940s one of our community, flying home from a reunion in the "Old Country" noticed that his hunger disappeared whilst airborne, but returned a few hours after he landed. He then tried it out flying round the world, well anyway within the limits of flights that were then available, and eating airline food, without ill effect – he didn't age, loose his hair, nails or teeth.

So up until "Lockdown" that's what a lot of us did. Have you ever wondered why first class and business seats are so often booked out – it's not because of "important businessmen/women" travelling to meetings, rather it's filled with members of the vampire community regularly travelling by plane to control their hunger. It's our way of fitting into modern life.

Airline food is great when you normally exist on a weekly pint of blood, and the *Sanguis Travel Monthly* regularly lists Emirates, Cathay Pacific, and Air India as the best airlines for vampires – provided you travel First or Business. I mean, where else can you get perfectly prepared steak tartare at 30,000 feet? Added to that the high ambient circulating CO_2 on an airliner seems to provide us all with a crackle of energy and a feeling of wellbeing. I'm sure there's a scientific explanation. OK, OK, go read up on the Bohr effect, but it certainly works for us!

Mind you a vampire must be careful when booking flights so that you leave early before sunrise and arrive at night! Flying to South America at least fits that bill.

So here I am, flying out on one of the first flights out of post-lockdown London, travelling to a Southern Hemisphere destination – it'll be winter when I arrive – for a temporary stay in a land of beef, tango, football, and good wine – long nights and a relatively Covid-free environment.

The Elders always complain that I'm too flippant about being a vampire, but when you've been around for a long time, you have to seek out the fun sides of this lifestyle, otherwise you'll end up as one of those dark twisted entities that they make movies about.

Sure there are downsides, what with the problems of a predominantly night time existence and all that blood and stuff, but sometimes you just have to make the best of it and enjoy yourself.

You know, I quite like this modern world; it's so much better than the Medieval and Victorian times, and don't get me started on about the last century, what with the wars, food shortages and rationing.

Today at least the world runs on a twenty-four hour clock, and with all this artificial lighting, at night everywhere is so brightly lit, so you can easily live a night-time life. On top of that you can now easily obtain your Vitamin D supplements, and get as much raw steak as you want, at all the supermarkets.

Well I'm certainly going to embrace this new millennium.

I suppose I could now say I was a Millennial Vampire?

Letter to Madelyn

My dear Madelyn,

I hope this letter finds you well. I suppose you really aren't – I mean who is going to be OK after being abandoned without a word at the Country House venue for our wedding?

I'm sorry not to have called either before or after the supposed wedding date but things got out of hand. It really was all the fault of my Best Man Gary who arranged a long weekend – well a week in Las Vegas for all ten of us – and all I can say it was great fun, but we got a little bit carried away. What little of that week I can recall was that I met a barmaid – Arlene that's her name – in the Millionaires Bar at the MGM Grand, and during the week of drinking, gambling and fun Arlene and I were married by Elvis in the Chapel of Love. I thought this was a joke, but I now know that this is totally official and sometime during the week I signed over all my assets and property to Arlene who promptly lost them on Red Seven at roulette. Now penniless Arlene and I have settled down in a Trailer Park on the edge of town and what's more Arlene is now expecting triplets.

What more can I say, except "Sorry"?

It was all sudden and unexpected and as I look back, I realise it wasn't such a bad decision; after all who wants to marry a billionaire fund manager's daughter or continue in a career as a professor of history at Oxford – as they say "Carpe Diem".

I write this from the CCU of Mercy Hospital in Las Vegas – the doctors say it's all the stress my 50-year-old body has experienced.

I don't suppose in memory of our friendship you could lend me $50,000 for my medical bills?

I wish you all the best and hope you remain in good health.

Yours as ever

Sam

First published on CaféLit 29 March 2022

A Journey Between Cities

The new Paris to Warsaw train service promised a smooth direct link for those wishing to cross Europe in relative comfort, free from airport delays, lost luggage, and painful waits at border controls. The fourteen-hour journey could be carried out in a relaxed manner, graced by good food, quiet carriages, and an ever-changing view. As ever the service run by Deutschen Bahn AG used the most advanced ICE-3 High Speed Train, which ran efficiently from Paris on a daily basis, with two main stops, at Frankfurt am Main and Berlin before terminating at Warsaw Central.

The invitation had arrived some weeks earlier, to give the opening address to the Warsaw Academy of Science with their offer to sort out all the travel and accommodation arrangements.

I had opted for the simplicity of the train to Warsaw rather than the shorter but more tedious flight from London to Warsaw. Sure, it involved taking the Eurostar from London to Paris but a two-day stopover in the City of Lights was a bonus before catching the seven o'clock train onwards to Warsaw. So, there I was settling into my first-class seat with plenty of reading material and audio books to occupy myself for the journey.

Minutes before the train departed the old man appeared, elegantly dressed in a pinstripe suit under a long grey coat topped off by a grey Fedora – an unusual feature in today's climate.

Taking the seat opposite me, he took off his coat, placed the old, battered briefcase he was carrying on the table between us, and neatly folded the coat, which he placed together with his hat in the rack above the seat. His movements were slow and controlled and somewhat sinuous for a man of his age. He sat down in the seat opposite and nodded to me.

Trying to be polite I nodded back and asked, "Are you going to Warsaw?" Stupidly I realised I'd spoken English and guessed he'd not understood, but surprisingly he replied in a soft middle European accent , "I certainly hope so – I've been trying to return for a long while, but this will be the first time I'll complete the journey."

He stood up and placed his old briefcase on top of his coat on the rack above him, carefully placing his hat on top of the case.

"Are you from Poland?" I asked, realising he wasn't as old as I'd first thought. He sat straighter in his seat and his face seemed less lined than it had first appeared.

"Oh, I left Poland a long time ago, and spent some time in Italy and France before settling down in London for many years" he replied.

He was interrupted by the carriage attendant, asking if we wished breakfast, which I accepted but he declined.

Breakfast was soon over and the train was now speeding through the French countryside as we rapidly closed in on the German border.

"I've never felt comfortable entering Germany," he said, "what with their history, especially towards the Poles, but I suppose we must put that all behind us."

"You know it seems we have something in common," I said. "My dad occasionally spoke about his father who, like you, had you left Warsaw but that was in August 1939 on a business trip and was never able to get back.

"Apparently, he ended up first in Italy, Trieste I think, and then went on to France. He joined the newly reformed Polish Army just before the German's invaded France and was finally evacuated to England in 1940."

The words kept tumbling out and I had no idea why I was telling a complete stranger this story about my grandfather, a man I had never met, but for some reason I felt compelled to finish the tale, so I rambled on.

"That was over eighty years ago, and my grandfather died when my dad was fourteen or fifteen, I think. Funny though, Dad always said that his father used to travel to Italy, and France – I can't recall which – every few months. Apparently, he was looking for a case or something he'd had to leave behind. I think Dad used to say that his father had got arrested and had to abandon a stash of diamonds that he'd smuggled out of Poland – but whether that was a joke, he never really knew, and couldn't ask him anyway."

It was all very odd, I'm usually pretty insular and rarely speak to people I don't know but somehow, I felt comfortable in the Old Man's company. Time passed and we rapidly crossed into Germany and stopped briefly at Frankfurt.

The lunch service came and went and as before the old man declined whilst I enjoyed the Beef Wellington – they wouldn't dare serve that in France but it was certainly OK in Germany.

The old man looked out at the German towns going past and appeared to shudder and again looked at me – for some reason I thought he looked younger, and his suit seemed to fit him better. I must be getting travel weary, I thought.

For a while we chatted amiably about the changing face of Europe, football, and my purpose in going to Poland.

"You know," the Old Man continued, "many years ago when I was living in London, I had a son but for a variety of reasons I never saw him grow up. We parted when he was a young boy and sadly, I never saw him again, but I think that if he had grown up, I would have liked him to be someone like you," he said looking at me, "but that was all a long time ago."

"Did you never try and contact him?" I asked – instantly

regretting the question. What business was it of mine? I don't know why, but I was intrigued.

"I tried on occasion," he replied, "but was unable to find him; it seemed he was lost to me."

It was an abrupt end to the conversation and now best avoided I thought.

The train thundered onwards towards Berlin. More coffee was served which the old man (seriously, was he now looking much younger?) again declined, and I realised that since we'd left Paris he'd not eaten or drunk anything on the train.

We pulled into Berlin station, roughly the halfway mark on the journey, and after a fifteen-minute stopover continued on our way towards the Polish border.

The continued motion of the train lulled me to sleep and when I awoke, I noticed that the old man was not sitting opposite, his old briefcase was on the table in front of me and looking up I saw that both his coat and hat were missing.

We were about an hour and a half out of Berlin, and the next stop was Warsaw Central in about five hours' time, so he couldn't have got off. I decided to give it a while hoping he'd return, before going to look for him and return his case, though somehow, I don't know why, I doubted I'd see him again.

He didn't return, so I started by asking the carriage attendants if they'd seen the old man leaving the carriage – his grey Fedora being a distinguishing feature – but they shook their heads. I must have gone up and down the full length of the train four or five times, even stopping to check the toilet compartments, but he was nowhere to be found.

I still had the old man's briefcase.

The train pulled into an underground platform at Warsaw Central Station, so grabbing my bag and the old man's briefcase I quickly alighted and remained standing at the bank of escalators taking passengers up to the main central concourse in the hope of catching sight of the old man but with no luck; he didn't appear amongst the arriving passengers.

Up on the central concourse I continued my search and thought I caught a glimpse of a grey Fedora; following I tried to catch up, but when the man briefly took of his hat, I saw he had blonde hair – certainly not that of the grey-haired old man from the train. Funny though, this youngish man was wearing an identical long grey coat and he carried a brown briefcase. I followed but the crowd surged, and I lost sight of him.

Still clutching the old man's briefcase, I turned and exited the station and took a taxi to my nearby hotel, The Polonia Palace, an old historic hotel that had somehow survived the Second World War, now beautifully refurbished and situated opposite the Warsaw Palace of Culture and Science, where I was due to give my address the following day.

Settling into my room, I contemplated about what to do about the briefcase. Open it and look for an address? Hand it in, either to the police or the lost property office at Warsaw Central on my return train trip?

Taking a deep breath, I opened the case and inside found only three items, including an old pre-war Polish passport dark blue and bearing the crowned Polish Eagle in gold. Inside there was no photograph just a name that had been partly obliterated but it still sent a shiver of anxiety through my body. No really?

What was impossible was also possible.

The earliest exit stamp was dated "Warszawa 18th August 1939", followed by a number of further stamps that included Ostrawa, Prague and Trieste all dated before the 1st of September 1939.

The second item was a gold metal "Wills Gold Flake" cigarette tin; you never see these nowadays, a real throwback to a bygone age. I carefully opened the tin and found four small velvet bags together with an old, faded cardboard ticket clearly marked Stazione di Trieste Central with a five-figure number printed on it. The velvet bags all clearly contained something or was it just rubbish? Carefully I opened the bags and poured out the contents, which clattered into the tin: forty diamonds of varying size sparkled in the base of the container, some were large and some slightly smaller; they all lay there reflecting the light.

Finally, I looked at the last item which was an old black and white photograph showing a youngish man lounging in a deck chair with a small boy seated at his feet smiling into the camera; the young boy I knew without doubt was my father, and the older man who bore a striking resemblance to the old man on the train could only be his father – my grandfather, a man who had died sometime in the early 1960s.

The photo was an exact copy of a large painting that had hung in my father's house, which he always claimed was a replica of a lost photograph that he had had of him and his father when they'd been on holiday when he was ten years old.

So, the old man, was he real? Had I dreamt my meeting with him? No that was impossible.

The journey was definitely real.

The briefcase was real; I had it in front of me.

The glittering diamonds were certainly real.

The photograph must be genuine.

So, who was the old man?

And where did he go?

Oh Wow! 2022

It happened again – and not just the once but repeated again and again at 1420 megahertz with a narrow bandwidth, each message lasting exactly seventy-two seconds with an intensity peaking at over twenty standard deviations higher than the background static.

The signals were picked up by the *Very Large Array Radio Telescope* in New Mexico, the *Alien Technology Array* at the Hat Creek Observatory in California, and the *Square Kilometre Array* in Western Australia.

The signal was identical to the one first observed in 1977 and again in 2020, that those bright sparks at the Big Ear Observatory at Ohio State had nicknamed the WOW! Signal.

The original signal had been tracked back to a region in the Constellation Sagittarius occupied by the star Tau Sagittarii. Well that was in 1977. The most recent signals emanated from the region of Tau Ceti, a Sun like yellow star in the Whale Constellation, Cetus, with four orbiting planets a mere twelve light years from Earth.

As one of the world's leading Astronomers succinctly put it, "It's in our own backyard!"

The astronomers, physicists and research teams around the world pored over the data attempting to understand and interpret the message with little result.

A team of Graduate students at the radio astronomy laboratory at the University of California, Berkeley had the bright idea of running the signal through the computers linked in with Caltech in Pasadena, and the images beamed to the various radio astronomy departments worldwide as well as the US Department of Defence and the Pentagon.

As the computer-generated image appeared, there was a global collective gasp as the world's leading Astronomers all stared at their computer displays, as a bright yellow smiley face clearly showing a thumbs up appeared on their numerous screens.

First published on CaféLit 31 March 2022

The New Hope v2.0

I have to leave; life here is too restrictive. The thought kept repeatedly coming into his mind. But how and where?

The pandemic had repeatedly recurred and returned; it had never really gone away. Time and again the European countries had gone into lockdown but always the virus came back. After six years there was still no completely effective vaccine, but as always there were rumours that one was imminent.

The US and other countries on the American continent had closed their borders, as had Russia and Belarus, both of whom were reporting as having mobilized their population into a "People's Army", and were now massing at their borders with the Baltic States, Finland and the Ukraine.

The European countries had likewise closed their southern and eastern borders to all non-Europeans and were violently preventing unauthorized entry into the European States.

Europe now resembled its pre-Second World War map of isolated separate countries with closed borders. The EU had failed in its first major test and all hopes of a great and powerful "United European State" had all but disappeared.

 The United Kingdom had now fragmented into a number of individual countries with restricted entry and little freedom of movement between them. Public transport had disappeared because of the lack of staff and the fear of travelling on the buses, trains or the various underground systems, the public were told, "Don't bother waiting for a bus; they are unlikely to come along either singly or in pairs."

The remaining public services in the United Kingdom had likewise almost disappeared. Rubbish piled up in the streets, the mortuaries were full, and staffing in hospitals had fallen well below critical levels. What remained of the health service existed only to provide an emergency service or care for those infected by the virus.

In the six years of the pandemic the British government had had six prime ministers just like Henry VIII wives, Resigned, Collapsed, Died, Resigned, Died, and Survived, but the government was very different. Now a Government of National Unity, there was no opposition and certainly no debate when the Threat to Health and Life Bill was passed.

This law gave the government complete control over all aspects of public and private life, effectively ending all public gatherings whether for sporting events, protest meetings or simply allowing the public or private meetings of more than six people. The police and the army were now effectively combined into a Civil Defence Force and were able to carry out detention and isolation of individuals through their Track and Trace powers.

British society had manifestly changed, with now over eighty per cent of the adult population on some form of government benefit or "furlough" payroll, with the government now controlling food, fuel, and the availability of medication.

Restaurants, shops, and pubs remained closed during the repetitive lockdowns and fewer and fewer were reopening as restrictions were repeatedly applied, relaxed, and applied yet again and again.

Many people had fled the cities and moved to the relatively uncrowded countryside, but that had changed. Property prices in the country towns and villages had skyrocketed and because of the pandemic you couldn't give away an inner city flat; and now caravan and tent cities had sprung up around many of these isolated towns and villages.

Only the promising glimmer of an effective vaccine

could reverse these many changes, but in the six years of the pandemic there had been four cycles of mass vaccinations, but still the pandemic waxed and waned and still the death toll throughout Europe kept rising.

Europe had become the very epicentre of the pandemic or Plague as the Russians were now calling it. The rhetoric building from Mother Russia and her allies was that Europe should be isolated, controlled and sterilised.

Now in attempt to silence the Russian chorus, the European Governments were announcing yet another mass vaccination program with a new anti-viral vaccine based on nanotechnology, which, if you now followed the numerous conspiracy theories would make you believe that this would further enhance government monitoring and allow the imposition of further restrictions on personal behaviour and freedoms.

He was lucky, he had survived the virus in its earliest first round and was one of the few lucky ones to develop antibodies and had seemingly remained immune throughout the last few years. Additionally, he had donated his antibody-rich plasma on a number of occasions, but after the third outbreak the local hospital had stopped asking, and despite repeated calls they had seemed uninterested, and had not got back to him.

On the positive side he'd been issued with a European and UK Biometric Bio Passport because of his immunity. The passport recognised throughout Europe and the United Kingdom (with the exception of Russia and Belarus) contained his immunity data, fingerprint, and retinal prints, as well as facial recognition, so could only be used by him and him alone.

Despite the many government controls, there were now numerous reports of isolated self-sustaining or "free communities" being set up all over Europe, well-armed and free of government control, but with little or no access to banking, medical or Wi-Fi services they nevertheless existed. Trying to find them would be problematic, but that's what he would do. He now knew of a number of "free communities" in West Wales and the Scottish Highlands and presumed there would be quite a few in the poorly populated but in the much less restrictive Scandinavian countries, far, far away from the epicentre of Europe.

Interestingly, whilst Denmark had stringent border controls between its southern European neighbours and at its maritime borders, the border between it and Sweden only existed during the phases of absolute lockdown, but once restrictions were relaxed there was little effective border control between the two countries, especially across the Oresund Bridge, which was the important road link between Denmark and Sweden across the Oresund Strait.

Over the last couple of years, he had progressively purchased small bars of gold, platinum, and palladium as well as a plentiful supply of gold sovereigns, krugerrands, salt, sugar pepper, and 100 litres of diesel in twenty litre Jerry cans. He still had his old shotgun and two boxes of cartridges; and he still had his two bows from his old archery days though only a dozen arrows, which were now becoming increasingly unavailable.

He'd taken the time and the trouble to research the best cold weather tent, for the cold Scandinavian winter weather, which he'd been able to directly purchase from its Alaskan supplier.

As the various lockdowns had eased, and temporary European travel had become possible, he had gradually ferried various items over to the lock-up garage he'd rented in Copenhagen, just back from the port area on the island of Zealand.

Also stored in the lock-up was the black four-year-old

Toyota Landcruiser he'd bought in Holland and driven directly to his Copenhagen garage; it was in good condition, less than thirty-five K on the clock and yes, only "one careful owner"! The beauty of the lock-up was that it was no distance from the E20 whereby he could easily access the Oresund Bridge, which put the sparsely populated regions of Sweden, Norway, and Finland within easy reach.

A twelve-hour drive could take him as far north as Trondheim in Norway or Ostersund in Sweden, but a shorter five-to-six-hour drive, just at the limit of a full tank in the Landcruiser) would take him to Varmland County with access to the huge area occupied by Lake Vanern, where the virus had had minimal impact.

So, as the lockdown was again eased in Europe in early April 2026, he packed up his old Mercedes, and from his home in a little village in Essex, drove via the Channel Tunnel, which had now reopened, to Copenhagen, essentially following the A1 and bypassing the still locked-down cities of Antwerp, Dortmund, and Hamburg.

He was allowed to pass through the many restrictive motorway and border controls by virtue of his passport and Bio Pass, but he knew that his data and journey was being logged on the various State databases.

The journey to Copenhagen took him over twenty hours and he had arrived at the lock-up in the early hours of the morning. He transferred what he'd transported with his Mercedes and loaded up the Land cruiser and settled down for a quick sleep. Six hours later fully refreshed, he took the Land cruiser, picked up the E20 and began his crossing into Sweden via the Oresund Bridge.

As he drove across the bridge toward Sweden he thought, maybe just maybe he could sit out the pandemic, or at least until it became totally controllable, within a "free community" and he could at some time return home to a more relaxed and much less restrictive and normal Britain. Well he truly, truly hoped so.

Halfway across the bridge the engine suddenly cut out, and he saw the blinding flash. The shockwaves rolled out from the epicentre of the explosion and he now knew that there was no hope, no future, and there would be no return.

Russia and her allies had begun their sterilization of Europe.

First published in *Aftermath*, Chapeltown Books, 2021

THeY

THeY stood watching in the corner of the square; the dawn was slowly breaking, and the hot moist night turned into an even hotter humid day. The mist rose lazily from the river obscuring their view of Algiers, and silently and still, THeY watched and waited.

The heat became oppressive and sweat trickled down their back soaking through the crumpled linen shirt, in the heat, mosquitoes and fat flies buzzed around, but still THeY watched and waited.

The quiet of the early morning was broken by the sound of the first tram of the day as it clattered and clanged its way along the riverbank, pausing at the far end of the square to disgorge it passengers. THeY could hear but not see the first ferry of the day lazily crossing the river to the island.

The hot sun continued to rise bathing the old square in bright sunshine, and more people began to arrive, seeking shelter along its shaded edges and a few brave vendors began to set up their stalls in the square, and in the heat of the day THeY silently watched.

The scream broke the silence and very soon THeY heard the wail of the sirens, and THeY knew that they had found their latest victim.

THeY felt no regret, no remorse just a brief lift of their spirits.

THeY had repeated this ritual weekly, hidden in the shadows around differing parts of the old city, always watching and waiting after the event, returning home to thankfully change out of the restrictive dark linen suit and white shirt THeY wore during their weekly ritual.

Only ever, during the spring and summer months when the hunger was greatest did THeY go hunting. Unsuspecting solitary men and women alone in the night were the victims dispatched without a sound. This was the fifth season of the hunt and still THeY had not been caught. Occasionally a witness would report seeing a dark clothed man leaving the area, but the police seemed unable to catch the culprit; they didn't even have a suspect. They'd even brought in experts from the FBI but still THeY eluded the law enforcement officers.

Around the city the police had put up their posters and nightly on TV and Radio they reported on the hunt for the "Spring Break Killer", so called because their first victim was found in Ponchartrain Park during Spring Break. The various descriptions of the suspect were vague at best: a slim man of average height and indeterminate age dressed in black. That was it. No facial features, no fingerprints, no DNA, nothing more, and so it had gone on for five years.

THeY had been very careful about not leaving clues, sometimes THeY wore a hat, sometimes a cap to hide their features and always, once sunrise occurred, wore large Ray Ban Aviator Sunglasses, and of course the surgical gloves.

Watching the crowd gather around the Police, THeY moved away, slipping off their jacket, partially unbuttoning their shirt, and removing the hat and sunglasses THeY casually strolled home to their flat in the Vieux Carré.

How long had it been? Seven years since the full transition, despite the hormones and subtle anatomical changes THeY still retained their original muscle strength.

As THeY changed out of their linen suit into something more comfortable and applied some fresh makeup, THeY realised the police could continue to look for the man they thought was the Spring Break Killer all they liked; they certainly weren't looking for a woman.

Time now to move on.

The West Coast looks promising.

First published on CaféLit 11 April 2022

One Small Drink for Mankind

The world watched and waited. The Probe had performed faultlessly and the trip using the Hoeman Transfer Orbit Calculator had taken precisely 260 days for the manned expedition to travel between Earth and Mars. Very soon the shuttle would descend from the mother craft to make the first manned landing on an orbiting planet of the Solar System.

The Mission Commander had carefully rehearsed his first words that he would say on setting foot on the red planet. NASA Mission Control in Houston would beam these words round the planet.

The shuttle landing went by the book, and after running all the requisite checks, which included the external camera settings, the moment of stepping out onto the surface had arrived.

The world watched as the Mission Commander opened the outer airlock door and slowly descended the steps to become the first man from Earth to set foot on the red planet.

As he stood on the unfamiliar surface, the Commander turned to face the camera and said, "Man has now become... wait a minute." He appeared to bend down and pick something up from the ground, which he thrust in front of the camera.

The twin golden arches could clearly be seen on the drink container.

"Cut the feed," screamed the NASA Flight Director, and speaking to the mission commander on the red planet, he calmly said, "Drop the cup and restart the speech; we'll handle it down here."

Nobody was really going to believe that the popular franchise had already opened on Mars ahead of NASA's first landing on the planet.

NASA Mission Control in Houston was glad of the nine-second time lag between receiving the images and transmitting them worldwide.

The Watchers

It was the first time they'd been back to Amsterdam for twenty years. They had met when they were postgrad students at the Free University; Guy was doing postdoctoral research on the wartime diamond trade between the Netherlands and Nazi Germany, and she was doing her PhD in International Law.

His Doctoral Thesis titled *Nazis, Diamonds and the Post War resurgence of Right-Wing Extremism* had been well received. For both it was love at first sight and as soon as Therese had received her doctorate they had married in Amsterdam. His doctorate opened many academic doors, and from Amsterdam they had moved to London for five years where he had been a lecturer in War Studies at Kings College whilst Therese had worked at one of the American banks in London.

London was followed by time at New York, Harvard and finally as Chairman of the Department of Conflict and Holocaust studies, and Director of the Hoover Institute at Berkley, California.

Therese likewise prospered and whilst they lived in New York had taken her Bar Exams and now in California was a partner in one of the Big Law firms specializing in International Banking Law.

The Archives of the Hoover Institute had been a treasure trove for his studies, and he had published four books and numerous academic papers on the funding and rise of right-wing extremist groups in Europe and their links with the illicit diamond trade, which had at its focal point the movement of diamonds between Rio de Janeiro and Amsterdam.

In January 2016 he was invited to become the Erasmus Visiting Professor in Modern History back at the Free

University in Amsterdam and would present the opening Address at the EU sponsored Congress on "European stability and the growing threat from Extremism". It would be a great idea to travel to Europe especially as their twentieth wedding anniversary would occur the day before the conference was due to start.

They drove from their home overlooking San Pablo Bay to San Francisco Airport in his old white Porsche convertible before taking the direct flight to Schiphol. On arrival they were met as they disembarked by a member of the EU sponsoring commission and were transported by a more sombre black Mercedes S500 to the Hotel American, that he had specifically requested.

The newly refurbished Hotel, which dated back to the 1930s, overlooked the Amstel and was sited not far from the Museums, diamond centre and the exclusive shopping streets of Amsterdam. The American Bar was claimed to be the best in the city and reputed to serve the finest Manhattans in Europe. The conference was due to commence two days after their arrival.

Their first day was spent reacquainting themselves with the sight and sounds of Amsterdam, hiring a couple of bikes and visiting some of the old coffee houses of the city. They were both amazed at the huge growth in the last twenty years of the number of houseboats that now lined the canals. Many of these had been individually designed and were positively luxurious. In the evening they were glad to see that the inhabitants of the city still continued with the habit of leaving their curtains and blinds wide open so passers-by could see directly into the living rooms.

That evening the EU Commission had invited the conference speakers and their accompanying partners to a late dinner at the ultra-chic restaurant "Le Garage", often frequented by celebrities, footballers, and politicians. What they both noticed as they were driven around the square in front of the Museum Quarter was a strangely silent candlelight protest of about a 1000 people dressed in black and carrying banners denoting the Dutch right-wing organisation, *Democratische Organisatie van de Oostelijke Reich* and surrounded by a similar number of silent riot police.

"I see the 'DooR' are still making their presence felt," he said to the accompanying EU Commissioner, Edouard. "This whole right-wing movement is spreading across Europe. Has this protest anything to do with the Congress?"

"I'm afraid so," replied Edouard. "You'll see them all over Amsterdam, dressed in black, wearing their red armbands."

Dinner at Le Garage was a great success, the escargots were truly amazing, and their main courses (pork for Therese and steak tartare for him) were the best they'd ever eaten. Leaving the restaurant, the guests almost walked into a dozen silent "Watchers" gathered outside, all dressed in black with their signature armbands. No words were exchanged though he noted that three of them were watching him intently as they walked to their car, one even smiling and nodding at him. Bloody strange.

The following day was spent at the Congress Centre meeting EU representatives, chairing a pre-Congress Workshop and meeting members of Europol who had a specific remit in monitoring Extremist Political Parties.

That evening which marked their wedding anniversary he had organised a private candlelight canal dinner cruise for the both of them, having arranged the exclusive private hire of the boat, chef, and crew of three.

The boat was waiting for them at the hotel's private jetty and as they boarded Guy noted two of the black clad members of 'DooR' watching them from just a few yards away. The table was set on the starboard side of the boat and Therese took her seat with her back to the bow whilst Guy faced forward. Her favourite aperitif of a Kir Royale was served to both of them; in truth he'd have preferred a whisky sour, but what the hell it was her day as well.

Over the next two hours the chef served a truly remarkable seven course "tasting menu" each dish served with a specially selected wine. The boat followed the one-way system imposed on the canal routes after dark. The canal-side was lit up as were the many bridges, but he noted that on almost every bridge along their route stood two of the watchers observing their leisurely progress. Like a guard of honour, Guy thought, as they drank their coffee and sipped their Cognacs.

The boat slowly turned off the main canal and followed one of the smaller waterways. Intrigued he glanced up and looked at a brightly lit-up three storey canal-side building with six brightly lit full-length windows, two to each floor. Standing in each of the middle two windows stood a single figure silhouetted by the bright light behind. The figures stood motionless, feet slightly apart and hands in their pockets clearly watching the progress of their boat. As the boat swung to the left, following the route of the canal, he was able to look directly at the brightly lit scene when suddenly the left-hand figure staggered and fell forward; a dark cloud formed on the window in front as the figure slid to the ground. Within seconds they had moved on and he lost sight of the building.

"Fucking Hell" he said to Therese. "Did you see that?

"See what?" she said.

"I think I've just seen someone being shot back there," Guy said, getting up and going forward to the captain, "and there's no fucking signal," he said looking at his phone.

"Captain," he said, "I think there's been a shooting back there and we need to call the police. Can we turn back?"

"I'm sorry Professor we can't turn around," replied the captain. "I'll bring the boat to a stop, and radio the police with our canal position. Are you sure of what you've seen?"

"Perfectly sure," Guy replied.

Within minutes a small police launch with its flashing blue lights appeared and helped both Guy and Therese aboard and slowly backtracked the cruiser's canal route, until they reached the canal-side location of the building where Guy had seen the shooting. As before all six windows were lit up. The middle-left window was partly obscured by a dark irregular stain covering the middle third of the glass.

"This is it!" shouted Guy, as one of the policemen spoke to his colleagues on the radio. "OK," he said, "they've located and entered the apartment, and would like you and your wife to join them." He guided the police launch to the canal-side.

The police escorted Guy and Therese to the large living room of the apartment on the middle floor, where police were grouped around a crumpled figure lying on the floor against the full-length window.

"Oh my God, it's Edouard!" exclaimed Therese.

"He's one of the EU Commissioners sponsoring our Congress," explained Guy, "an expert on Right Wing Extremism within the EU and he was going to give a paper on the 'DooR' at the congress later today."

"Thank you, Professor," replied one of the police officers. "I'm Commissioner van Rijn and I'll be handling the investigation."

Guy noted that the policeman had a red badge on his left lapel, which without his glasses he thought he could make out the letters D...o...o...R embossed on it. Gazing over the commissioner's shoulder and through the window

Guy could see a half dozen "Watchers" standing together on the opposite side of the canal all looking up at the window. He realised that all the policemen in the room wore identical badges. There was absolutely nowhere to go, nowhere to run to; even the police seem to be involved.

"It is a real pity that you were a witness to the recent proceedings," said the Commissioner, as he reached into his jacket.

First published in *Tales from the Upper Room*, Bridge House, 2017

The Dog in a Bag

The dark clothed man first appeared walking along the boulevard by the old town of Menton on the French Riviera. Tall and elegant wearing a floppy hat to protect him from the afternoon sun he strolled with a relaxed gait and carried a large bag which, when he sat at the harbour café, clearly revealed a sleeping dog curled up in the bottom of the bag. Ordering a *pression* he languidly lit up a cigarette and the dog lazily raised its head to look over the edge of the bag, its red eyes looking out at the press of people passing by. He patted the dog's head and whispered calming words. The dog settled back into its bag and the man continued to sip his drink.

The late afternoon turned into early evening and still the man sat in the café, the dog slumbering in the bag. A tumultuous barking from a number of nearby dogs shattered the early evening peace and a crowd suddenly surrounded a fallen tourist who lay face down in an ever-enlarging crimson pool. The man stood up to survey the scene and the dog raised its head from the bag as did a second identical head and then a third head; the dog with three heads stood up from the bag and leapt into the crowd.

The three headed dog Cerberus had come to claim another soul for his master Hades.

———————————

First published on CaféLit 4 May 2022

Martha

It was 10 am in the morning and Martha Strang looked out over the waterfront as the shutters were raised on her bar on the Rambla overlooking the River Plate. As usual she checked that the four back tables of the bar had their chess boards and figures laid out ready for the old émigrés who came to play in the dark shaded reaches of Martha's bar.

Harry, her barman, business partner and closest friend, was busy cleaning glasses and checking that the coffee machine was warmed up and ready to serve endless cups of Café Largo, along with the day's delivery of Medilunas – the sweet Uruguayan version of a croissant.

Unlike in other bars, the background music was always classical and often based upon the many ballets she loved, those by Tchaikovsky, Prokovief and Stravinsky being her favourites.

The sun was up and burning bright and it was on days like this that the tattooed stars on her chest itched, a reminder of the time spent at the notorious IK14 prison in Mordovia – a god-forsaken land southeast of Moscow.

It was there in the prison in Mordovia that Martha or as she was called then, Marta Mikhailovka Stranny, had served fifteen years for drug smuggling and theft. It was only after the fall of the Soviet Union that she had been allowed her freedom, and the ability to move to South America, where with the help of her "friends" she had opened her bar on the Montevideo waterfront.

Those friends – all of whom, like her, had stars tattooed on their chest, and in some cases on their knees with the message "I kneel to nobody" – had helped her forge close links with the large Italian immigrant community, as well as providing a safe haven for the many of her countrymen who had also left Russia to take advantage of the many opportunities available in the southern reaches of the Americas. She like the many émigrés had no desire to return home to either Mother Russia or a Russian prison.

Uruguay, a small prosperous South American country, was often ignored by many of those crime agencies such as the US Drug Enforcement Agency, Interpol, and Europol, and was now providing a fruitful source for the ever-increasing cocaine market in Europe.

The drug itself was being smuggled out of the country by Italian and Russian "businessmen" to their Italian colleagues in Naples and Calabria. This was enabled by the total lack of Customs Control and Supervision in many of the South American ports.

Martha's bar had served as a central meeting place where, deals were made, and shipments arranged. Martha herself, with Harry's help, had acted as a broker between the interested parties to ensure a smooth transfer of the drugs to Italy and guaranteed that cash flowed in the opposite direction.

Martha had risen in the Russian Brotherhood both before and after her imprisonment and had earned her stars of seniority whilst in prison.

Following her trial her husband had fled the Soviet Union with their daughter and had disappeared for a while, though information had come to light that he had settled in the US Midwest. Their daughter, had grown up as a US citizen, graduated in law and was now working in the US Attorney General's Office.

Martha had tracked down her husband to Boise, Idaho and had sent him a message of intent via a Chechen Boyevik, a warrior. Her daughter, however, remained unreachable.

By midday the bar was half full. At the back a number of older men were sipping coffee, playing chess, and smoking Papirosu – the old-fashioned filter-less Russian cigarette. Sometimes Martha would join them in a game of chess, but not today.

Promptly at one o'clock four Russians entered the Bar and after greeting them, Martha asked Harry to show them up to the meeting room above the bar whilst she waited patiently for the remaining members of the group to arrive.

After a wait of a few minutes four more middle-aged men entered and speaking in heavily accented Italian Martha welcomed the men representing their Italian partners and led them upstairs.

She seated herself at the head of the table, whilst the eight men took their places, helped themselves to drinks and coffee and discussed the next series of shipments to Europe, agreeing prices, delivery dates and cash deposits. The talks were friendly, no disagreements, and all agreed that as long as the supplies continued, and the various Uruguayan politicians and Senior Police Officers were adequately compensated then a peaceful coexistence could continue.

The quiet calm of the afternoon was shattered by an explosion in the downstairs bar and the meeting room door burst open as six armed members of the Policía Nacional entered all with their guns pointed at the seated group around the table; standing, Martha noted that one of the red laser beams was firmly focused on her chest. The balaclava wearing policía were followed by four civilians all wearing body armour and black caps bearing the logo of the DEA – the US Drug Enforcement Agency.

One of them a female that Martha thought she recognised but couldn't remember from where, approached her saying in perfect Russian, "Hello, Mama; it's good to see you again after so long."

First published on CaféLit 20 July 2022

The Cheese Sandwich Dilemma

The trouble with time travel is that it is full of dilemmas. You go back in time. Is it your past or an alternate reality past and the same thing when you travel forwards in time; whose future is it or when is it?

Those scientists working in the Transient Particle Unit where they'd originally identified the tachyons, together with "High Energy" and "Sterile Neutrinos" spent a lot of time pondering this dilemma. These researchers had first noted that those particles both appeared and disappeared instantaneously, and their mathematical calculations and modelling inferred that the particles were able to travel both backward and forward in time. So, the theory was that if you bombarded an object with these transient particles depending on their velocity you could propel an object either backwards or forwards in time.

The Cheese Sandwich Test was the basis for time travel. In their first series of tests the scientists were able to send a Cheese Sandwich (mature Cheddar if you ask) backward in time, initially for ten seconds, then for longer periods of time and finally for twenty-four hours.

How did they know this? Well, they sent it back to their own lab where the scientists had already logged the arrival time of the sandwich, which they already knew, as it had already happened anyway.

Are you following this so far?

Now the important thing, dear readers, is that each sandwich was freshly made before being sent back in time, so it was whole when it left and whole when it arrived. So, the cheese sandwich, as it bounced back in time, followed a coherent timeline – it was made, sent back in time, and returned to its original timeline intact and as fresh as it was when sent.

Confidently the scientists turned their attention to the exciting prospect of the transportation of the cheese sandwich into the future.

So, they repeated their tests sending the cheese sandwich ten seconds, ten minutes, and ten hours into the future – smooth as silk. It was when they got more adventurous and started sending the cheese sandwich further and further into the future, that they hit the dilemma.

A cheese sandwich was sent two weeks into the future; it departed smoothly and immediately returned to the point of origin with a large bite taken out of it.

So, the team shut down their experiment, and waited for the two weeks to elapse until the whole cheese sandwich they'd sent into the future appeared, which it did – a perfect cheese sandwich with a bite taken out of it. The partially eaten sandwich appeared, shimmered, and disappeared back into the past.

OK folks so answer me this: how can a cheese sandwich made fresh today and sent into the future as a whole sandwich return to its past with a bite taken out from the future – was it/is it the original sandwich? Or where did it go and who or what bit into the cheese sandwich?

The scientists could only conclude that somewhere floating around in the universe of time there is a whole cheese sandwich waiting to be eaten.

First published on CaféLit 23 July 2022

The Old Man

Paris 1932

The old man – well he really wasn't that old – sat in the corner of the bar, his black moustache covered with the foam of the beer he was drinking. His dark blue suit was somewhat crumpled, and he lit up another cigarette as soon as he stubbed out the previous one.

He nodded to me and waved me over. "Come, and take a seat. We're two strangers here in Paris, join me for a drink."

He seemed an amiable fellow as we chatted about the recent football results; he was a keen supporter of Schalke, the North Rhine team. Me? I followed The Arsenal of course.

We talked about the motor racing and the success of the Auto Union-Mercedes team the Silver Arrows, and discussed the forthcoming Olympics, which he seemed quite excited about.

"We're hosting it you know, the Olympics that is, and we're preparing a Games that'll astonish the world, and certainly give those decadent jazz loving Americans something to think about."

"So what brings you to Paris?" I asked.

"Just a trip, to see the so-called Cultural Capital of Europe, but it doesn't really compare with home," he replied.

"I'm certainly going to return here to Paris very, very soon, maybe with more of my colleagues and friends.

"I'd love to show them the sights of the city: the Eiffel Tower, Notre Dame, and the Louvre," and jokingly he added, "Maybe even march through the Arc de Triomphe with some of them. That would be fun!

"I do so like to visit these old European capitals, but sadly none can really match up to any of our own cities." He paused, and then added, with his voice rising an octave or two, "Maybe we should try and bring some of our culture and order to these excessively liberal European cities, their inhabitants seem to lack the moral restraint of my countrymen.

"And you?" he asked.

"Like yourself just a simple visit; I'm just a humble Englishman touring Europe," I replied. "Seeing Paris, then off to see Rome, Vienna and Warsaw."

"Interesting," he added smiling. "Rome, the so called Eternal City, you'll love it; as for Vienna, you know, I used to live there and do some painting, but that was a while ago.

"But you know what; what I'd really, really like to do is visit Poland," he mused. "Never been there, but I hear that since '21 it's become such a large country, with so much more space, maybe, maybe I'll visit it.

"No, I certainly must visit it, soon maybe, definitely within the next couple of years, possibly sooner, if everything goes according to plan."

We were interrupted by the arrival of two men dressed in black.

"Alas I must leave." He handed me a card, and said, "Maybe we can meet again sometime soon; come and join me for a weekend at my country place in Obersalzberg before you return home."

One of the men stepped forward and clicking his heels said, "Mein Führer, your car awaits."

The Night Train to Hue

At his colleague's invitation he took the night train to Hue. He hadn't been back since '68. the last memories he had of Hue was being airlifted out flat on his back on a stretcher attached to the side of a "Slick", officially the transport version of a Bell UH-1 Iroquois helicopter affectionately known as a Huey. He could remember the thumping sound of the helicopter blades and the painted coiled black snake on the nose of the Huey.

He was nineteen at the time. His unit the 5th Battalion 7th Cavalry, had been rushed into Hue to try and retake the southern perimeter of the Citadel that had been taken by the People's Army at the start of the Tet Offensive. They had travelled to the Old Imperial City along Highway One where their force of 300 men supported by other troops from the 1st Cavalry Division and ARVN units were to engage with over 7000 men of the People's Army of North Vietnam, who had, in a surprise attack, occupied most of Hue and taken the old Imperial City often called the Citadel by the US forces.

As dawn broke and the train rattled along, he looked out of the carriage window and figured that the road that the railway track ran alongside must be that self-same Highway One that had taken him and his comrades to the Imperial City of Hue all those years ago.

He remembered that they had ridden to the Citadel in APCs, the lightweight vehicles travelling at over forty mph which were both fast enough to evade the intermittent artillery fire and sufficiently armoured to protect the passengers from small arms fire. His memories of that time were a blur, but he clearly remembered the hit, the surprise, the pain, the shock and lying on his back; he remembered being dragged towards the thumping sound of a helicopter, some pain relief from the

118

morphine syrette jabbed into him, and the slow ascent into the sky, as he was transported out to the nearest field hospital. He would later find out it was the 95th Field Hospital sited on Red Beach, Da Nang.

Confusion, pain, disorientation, and operations all quickly followed. Then followed an airlift out, firstly to Tokyo, then Hawaii and finally to the Walter Reed Hospital in Washington, via Los Angeles and Minneapolis. Each stop was associated with a sea of pain, drugs, and rehab, but he'd made it through, been discharged from the army, and under the GI Bill went off to University and Medical School, and a Surgical Residency completed at the self-same Walter Reed. Academic appointments followed and he'd finally settled into his role as a full Professor of Surgery at a Mid-Western University.

For all these years other than attending various meetings within the US, he had preferred to stay in his own mid-western state, choosing to enjoy his down time fishing, sailing on the state's many lakes, and camping out in the northern wilderness.

His trip to Hanoi was the first time that he'd left the US since returning home from 'Nam many years ago. Taking the flight out of O'Hare in Chicago, he flew the first leg to Tokyo and then onwards to Hanoi. It was the right time and the right thing to do at this stage of his life.

Hanoi was now a modern city, the centre full of glass and steel, but nestled amongst the new structures were the tall narrow buildings of pre-war Hanoi. The roads were packed with cars and motor scooters, many balancing whole families or the contents of a market stall on them as they weaved their way through the endless traffic. The many coffee houses still served the original coffee made with condensed milk and added egg for the true Hanoi version.

His visit to Hanoi was at the invitation of the Chief of Surgery at the Hanoi Medical University, with whom he'd corresponded over the years and had met on a number of occasions at meetings in the US.

He'd spent the previous couple of weeks helping set up a minimal access surgical laboratory to hone the skills of the next generation of Hanoi trained surgeons.

Like him the Professor was a 1000-day veteran having served with the People's Army and now they were both travelling to Hue, not by car or plane but by the overnight train now christened the "Reunification Express". The first-class carriages had four berths and they were lucky enough to secure all four as a "Private `Berth" so only the two of them occupied their particular cabin.

As his surgical colleague had said, it would have been all too easy to fly from Hanoi to Hue but why not take the train, a thirteen hour adventure on the old French narrow-gauge railway that in many places paralleled Highway One.

They had departed the capital from the now featureless and rebuilt Hanoi Central Station under the watchful gaze of the blue uniformed train officials; the men still wore the classical Vietnamese high-peaked hats and the women, he was happy to note, wore a much more flattering uniform.

The train was packed with families and backpackers, as they noisily crowded out of their berths and spilled out into the carriageway, constantly making way for food carts and drink trollies that seemed to go endlessly up and down the train; this was in stark contrast to US trains, as on the "Reunification Express" there was a complete absence of a buffet car or restaurant.

The passengers on the train exhibited the multi-ethnic composition of the Vietnamese people, with those from the northern Chinese border, freely mixing with families from the Cambodian regions and Central Highlands, as well as their southern cousins, many en route to Saigon or "Ho Chi Minh City" as it was now called.

During the trip, he and his Vietnamese colleagues, whose mastery of English was excellent, had plenty of time to chat, compare histories and memories of their time spent in their respective armed forces.

For the Vietnamese it was a matter of patriotism, loyalty, and purpose, but simply put, they had little option to being drafted; and the Vietnamese professor had played his role in the 5th Regiment of the People's Army of Vietnam.

As for the US professor, he had volunteered straight out of High School, following a route previously taken by his father, grandfather, and great grandfather, who had all done their bit starting with the Civil War, through WWI and WWII and now it was his turn. He had been drafted into the 1st Cavalry Division (Airmobile) better known as "The Aircav" and mustered into Custer's old regiment the 7th Cavalry.

Both men had participated in the siege of Hue on either side of the battle that had ensued during the Tet Offensive of 1968. At one point they surmised that they might have faced each other during the US assault on the Citadel. No animosity was felt; the futility of the war and time, had healed their wounds, and the old comrades in arms respected each other and had clearly moved on with their lives.

The train journey progressed as all train journeys do; numerous stops at towns and villages, the changing nature of the country, sunset, night, and dawn passed. The boisterous noise and the constant movement of passengers up and down the carriageway never really ceased.

They ate "Pho", the traditional beef noodle broth in the evening, and the "Banh Mi" breakfast sandwich as dawn broke.

Sunrise brought images of a relatively unchanged landscape of rivers, streams, water buffalo, and still had that classical appearance that had so often been seen on the endless TV newscasts. The water buffalo standing in the rice fields and rivers, and the workers in the fields wearing their distinctive conical hats or "nón lá", the vista shaded orange by the rising sun.

Finally, after thirteen hours they arrived at Hue, where they were met by a number of the professor's old students, now established as surgeons in the old City of Hue and nearby Da Nang.

The group drove across the Perfume River to have brunch at the well-known *Les Jardins de Carambole* – an old French restaurant on the southwest corner of the Citadel, and as they crossed the river the US professor had thought that this was likely to have been the self-same bridge, they had used to access the Old City all those years ago. His platoon had been one of the last units to use the bridge before it was heavily damaged in the offensive.

Brunch was conducted in a mixture of Vietnamese and English over a variety of local and excellently made European dishes, with its members gradually disappearing off to pursue their daily commitments. Finally, it was just the two of them.

"Come," said his Vietnamese colleague, "I've something of interest to show you before we have a look at the Imperial City."

Leaving the restaurant, they walked along the road that paralleled the southern perimeter of the Citadel, until they reached a sign that read *Thua Thien History Museum*. "I think that what you're seeking is just over there," he said, pointing to a row of tanks and helicopters.

There alongside a variety of large, US tracked vehicles, were a couple of Hueys which he instinctively knew were the transport "slicks" used to ferry the badly injured out of the battlefield. Approaching, he noted that one of them had the faded image of a coiled black snake on its nose and going closer he stepped up and grasped the right-hand side rail onto which he'd been strapped all those years ago.

He closed his eyes, and he could clearly hear the thump of the helicopter rotor blades and then images and memories of his life seemed to go backwards first slowly and then more rapidly: the trip, his many surgical procedures, the fishing trips, his residency, his college days, then Washington, Minneapolis, Los Angeles, Tokyo, and Da Nang, all the while with the noise of the rotors in the background.

Opening his eyes, he found he was lying back on the stretcher strapped onto the side rails of the Huey clearly marked with a coiled black snake. He could hear the sound of small arms fire punctuated by loud explosions and all the while the thump of the Huey's rotor blades. His vision became blurred, and he was tired, so tired, his vision dimmed, and he closed his eyes for the last time.

Once We Were Heroes

There had been six of us; we'd survived all these years and only a few people in the Pentagon had known our true history. A close-knit band of enhanced professionals deployed wherever and whenever we were needed, supported by our high-tech specialist equipment.

Under the Classified Presidential Order our existence and deployment was both ultra-secret and totally deniable. As the years went by as members of the group died, it was my job to go into their homes to remove any evidence of our secret lives. In reality I was guardian of their top-secret legacy.

Jack Lovell had been the first to pass; his bright star had flamed out at the turn of the century and was soon followed by Bruce, a gentle giant of a man built like a brick outhouse, his heart unable to cope with his powerful frame.

The old man of the sea, Roman Prince, had drowned doing what he loved: surfing in Hawaii, and Blake Odinson, with the government's blessing, had returned home to take over his father's business, but I hadn't heard from him for many years.

Only Daniel and I were the known surviving members of the group until I got the call that Daniel had died and again it was my job to check and clear his apartment.

Frankly I was surprised that Daniel (he hated being called Danny) had made it this far.

Following our military deployment in the early 60s he'd suffered a severe chest injury that had damaged his heart, but with his engineering skills and genius had developed an advanced technology that allowed him to not only survive but also boosted his strength and his intellectual capability. His penthouse flat in New York was clean and tidy and superficially there was no evidence of his past life as an enhanced super soldier. The safe was empty of any incriminating documents but I knew that behind his clothes closet was a hidden secret compartment that of course I knew how to open, well I was a super soldier too, and Daniel's oldest and closest friend.

The compartment door slid open and there they were, Daniel's old battle suits, the original gold one, and the newer black and silver suit, plus a briefcase, which contained just three items, a comic, a photo, and an envelope with my name printed on the front. The photo showed our group of six before our first deployment in 1962, Young, fit, and ready to go. The comic was a *Tales of Suspense* issue from 1963 introducing a silver-suited Iron Man.

I opened the letter, which read:

Dear Matt,

If you're reading this, I know you're cleaning up the apartment. They were fun years when we all worked together for the government, and I always knew you'd outlive us all – I mean you haven't aged a day; I guess it was that serum they gave you back in the 50s. Keep the photo safe; it's the only copy that exists – all the others plus the negatives were destroyed. For a laugh see the comic; they couldn't even get the name and the battle suit right, but I'm surprised the government still let it through the censors in '63 – keep it safe.

I know you're still working with the government alongside our old boss Max, so keep the Shield close and stay safe.

Your old friend Daniel.

I put the items back in the briefcase and signalled to the yellow-jacketed "Cleaners" that it was OK to clear the apartment. I took the briefcase and left. I never wear the red, white, and blue they dressed me in years ago – jeans and a leather jacket suffice. The shield is stowed in the trunk of the Bentley that Daniel gave me. Their legacy will probably survive in the comics, and I now hear they're thinking of making a film about our early exploits – but who'd ever believe it?

Back Pain

The back pain had been a constant feature of his life for the last few months. Normally he was a fit man, going to the gym on a daily basis; he ate healthily and walked everywhere, but now he was getting less and less mobile. In the last couple of months his normally grey hair had turned white, his posture had changed and the back pain was relentless. The persistent pain was located up between his shoulder blades, and he found it difficult to get comfortable in bed and sitting in a chair was miserable. He'd visited his GP who put it down to arthritis and old age and told him to take some anti-inflammatory painkillers. A scheduled appointment at the local hospital was eighteen months away so he decided to go "private" as they say. Unfortunately he was not privately insured so he figured it was going to cost him an arm and a leg, but so what if it got rid of the pain; he'd sort out his finances, sell the car or cash in part of his pension.

The private consultation with the specialist was as expected: "We'll organize some tests such as X rays, MRI of spine, get a few bloods and organize some," intoned the consultant; he seemed to be reading from a script, *Back pain 101.*

"Not sure why your hair has gone white," the consultant added; maybe it's a vitamin or magnesium deficiency which could be linked with the back pain; let's look into it when we've got the blood and MRI results."

Dutifully he went off and had his X Rays, MRI and a whole host of bloods, which included something called a metabolic profile. His next appointment was a couple of weeks away and during that time his back pain increased. One night when he tried to settle into his favourite armchair he found he couldn't fully lie back as the curvature of his spine had increased. Looking in the full length mirror in his

127

bedroom – he was now having to walk upstairs almost on all fours – he thought he could see what looked like two bony protrusions between his shoulder blades. What the Hell?

At his next appointment the consultant looking at the X Rays and MRI. "Never seen anything like this. It looks like you've got new bone growth forming alongside your thoracic spine that appears to be growing outwards from the spine. I'm going to refer you to the Royal National Orthopaedic Hospital at Stanmore; I'm sure they can figure this out and deal with it appropriately. If I didn't know better I'd say you were growing vestigial wings.

"By the by, your blood results are all OK, so I'll pop a referral to a dermatologist in the internal mail and see if they can give you some idea as to why your hair has turned white, but don't hold your breath."

By the time he was seen by the specialists at Stanmore the bony protuberances had significantly enlarged and had now penetrated his skin giving him an appearance of having two spikes on his back. The specialists could shed no further light on the problem, other than this was a benign condition, possibly some form of genetic bony growth and yes they did look like vestigial wings, and yes they'd be happy to remove the bony growths. Come back in a month once you've had time to think about this and we can organize the operative treatment; meanwhile here were some helpful booklets on *Managing Back Pain, Your Back Operation and What To Do After Your Operation.*

As he travelled back, he was lost in thought, debating the issue of an upcoming operation. Arriving home he noticed that propped up by his front door was a long tall parcel encased in its distinctive Amazon packaging.

"Wasn't expecting anything," he mumbled to himself. He looked at the label and clearly saw that it was addressed to him with the correct address. There it was on the label: Mr M. D'Angelo. There was no doubt that it was for him.

Opening it the Archangel Michael drew out his flaming sword from the Amazon packaging as his wings finally burst through his clothes and spread out.

First published on CaféLit 12 May 2023

A New Mexican Adventure

They had cracked the problem of interstellar space travel. Well they thought they had. An additional bonus was that the model they used also removed the problem of relativistic time dilation by using captured tachyons and the application of the Alcubierre Drive.

The Mexican physicist Miguel Alcubierre had first proposed the Drive, in 1994; it postulated that the ship would sit in a relativistic-free warp bubble whilst the space ahead was flattened, folded, and shortened. In simple terms both Earth and the ship's crew would experience the same time lapse for the journey (and return) without the effects of relativity. So, if the journey to the star, irrespective of the distance in light years, took three months as experienced by the ship's crew, only three months would have elapsed on Earth. The energy needed for the drive was immense, but the identification and capture of tachyons solved the energy problem. Thus, the spacecraft could move at supra light speed merely by folding space, and it would put most of the star systems of the Milky Way galaxy within easy reach, well at least within a five-year period of travel.

They had identified an earth-like planet orbiting the star Kepler 1649-c with a mass comparable to that of the Earth, a similar period of rotation, and an orbit of 1.06 years around the main star. The planet lay within the Planetary Goldilocks zone (not too hot, not too cold), and the Star itself exhibited features identical that of Earth's own sun.

They calculated that the trip to Keppler 1649-c would take forty-two days and a six-man team would make the journey to the identified planet. Once inside Kepler's system the spacecraft would de-accelerate and orbit the planet at 250 miles. The de-acceleration and orbit would add a further thirty days to the journey.

There was a four-man landing craft available, if the Mission Commander thought it appropriate, but because of the distances involved the team were essentially alone and out of contact with Earth. Messages based on tachyon bursts would still be affected by the physics of relativity, making interstellar communications useless.

The international crew consisted of a mission commander who was an astrophysicist from Albuquerque New Mexico, an astro-navigator, two exobiologists (at least, that's how the Mission defined them), a medically qualified biologist and a flight commander who was also a theoretical physicist. All members of the crew would also be able to fly and navigate the spacecraft back to home if absolutely necessary. The exobiologists were trained to both fly the landing craft, and effect take-off and docking with the main spacecraft if necessary.

The spacecraft, named after the Mexican physicist who first proposed the interstellar drive, was *The Miguel Alcubierre*. It was launched from its Earth orbit and once past the moon accelerated north of the plane of the Solar System and switched on its tachyon drive.

The ship re-entered the Solar System 144 days after launch and took a further twenty-five days to achieve a stable Earth orbit to enable docking with the Global Earth Space Station. Only the flight commander and the navigator were on board.

In his report the flight commander stated:

"The flight to Kepler 1649-c went as smoothly as predicted and we were able to take up a stable orbit at precisely 250 miles above the designated planet. There were no radio transmissions or communication from the planet, which had two main continents. Atmospheric sampling revealed an oxygen-rich atmosphere with less than three percent carbon dioxide, and seventy-five percent nitrogen. The smaller of the two continents appeared uninhabited, but there was evidence of a significant population on the larger continent. Visual imaging together with infrared and ultraviolet spectroscopy revealed that the population consisted of humanoid type inhabitants, clustered around large centres of habitation. The designated four-man landing party took the drop ship to the nearest large 'city' with the hope of establishing contact, and apart from a very brief message, presumably from their vocal implants, we lost all contact. The message was partially interrupted by some form of static interference, though we've been able to clean it up as best we can. We remained in orbit for a further thirty days but were unable to re-establish contact with the landing party; we've left three communication beacons in orbit and if they are able to re-establish communication, though it's a long shot but if so, the triggered tachyonic burst would reach this Space Station in approximately twelve years."

The flight commander played the communication burst from the landing party:

"…Landed OK, we were met by humanoids just like us, but they destroyed the ship…

"…Removed our flight suits… Air is breathable… They're taking us to a building that looks like the Aztec temples you see in Mexico …"

"After that, all communication was lost," said the flight commander, "and as I said, we stayed on station for a further thirty days but heard nothing more…"

He continued, "The planet seems perfect for colonization except for the natives. I think we should mount a further trip back to the Kepler system, but this time we must be accompanied by well trained and heavily armed troops."

So, some six months later a new mission commander

accompanied by the original flight commander and navigator led "Operation Hernan Cortes" (named after the Spanish adventurer who conquered the Aztec Empire in Mexico), to the planet Kepler 1649-c.

The mission, now heading into vast blackness of space, was accompanied by a battalion of the newly formed space marine division nicknamed "The Conquistadores" because of their distinctive space armour; their divisional motto was "He travels safest in the dark night".

Some joker in the Mission Planning Committee declared it was a case of an "old Mexican warrior enabling a New Mexican adventure".

As before, the trip and the necessity of establishing a stable planetary orbit took just over three months of relative time, and finally, after arriving at the planet, three drop-ships, each carrying a company of the heavily armed Conquistadores, landed on the planet.

As the troops disembarked, and as they formed up in their companies ready to wreak havoc upon the planet's inhabitants, much as their predecessors had done hundreds of years ago, a huge silent crowd of aliens met them. The crowd stretched back from the Conquistadores landing site to the very edge of the alien city where their colleagues had previously landed.

The marines led by their commanders now accompanied by the flight commander and navigator of the original expedition slowly advanced to the edge of the city as the crowd parted to form an unobstructed avenue for their progress. The silent alien-lined avenue, like the waters at the sea edge ebbed and flowed as the aliens constantly took up new positions to guide the armed warriors to the very edge of a city centre pyramid shaped building with a wide central staircase leading to the very top. The building as described by the first landing party in its brief communication was similar – no, identical, thought the flight commander – to those Aztec Temples of old.

At the base of the pyramid the advancing men were met by six aliens, all wearing ornate robes and what looked like feathered headdresses.

They look exactly like us thought, the Flight Commander, as the aliens gestured upwards.

The Flight Commander, Navigator and a Company Commander began to ascend the pyramid, following the long staircase to the very top accompanied by a company of armed Conquistadores.

There at the very top seated around a long table were the missing men of the original mission, accompanied by a number of the aliens, all robed, all wearing headdresses and all drinking what the flight commander thought must be some kind of local spirit. As they reached the top, the original mission commander stood stretched out his arms saying, "Welcome comrades, welcome to what we've called Nuevo New Mexico; sit, and drink with us. Not sure what it is but sure tastes like tequila. We have much to tell."

As their tale unravelled, the men of the original expedition gave an account of an alien spaceship from this very planet landing in Central America some two millennia ago, settling amongst the local population who regarded them as "Gods." For many hundreds of years the aliens lived peaceably amongst the native earthlings, building their society and civilization and intermarrying with the locals. Biologically humans and aliens were identical, and as one of the exobiologists explained – life in the universe has a way of repeating itself; after all as he said, "We're all composed of the same atoms formed from the same constituents that are all part of the universe."

"Like us these humanoid aliens, are apex predators;

they're always bipedal, with two arms and a muscle mass that is able to carry its owner efficiently over varying surfaces, always with binocular vision. It is likely, that planet-to-planet, constellation-to-constellation, the apex predator will be identical; after all we're all composed of the same atoms, molecules and protein chains that are all part of the same universe. What does differ is their immune response and susceptibility to disease, but in the almost closed society of the then Mayan civilization – not the Aztecs – this didn't seem to matter."

The exobiologist continued, "There was a time when the descendants decided to return to their home planet and took with them their families, slaves and others. Like us, the Aliens – should we still call them that? – chanced upon their own version of the Alcubierre Drive, which allowed them to fold space. It was their return that finally did for the original civilization here on this planet that we call Keppler 1649-c. In the intervening years since the original ship had departed Keppler, the planet had been affected by internecine and religious wars, disease, starvation and a partial collapse of civilization, made worse with destruction of their libraries, universities and scientific institutions. This fall was compounded by the returnees arrival back from Earth, which brought with it unknown viruses and diseases from Earth to which the planet's inhabitants had no resistance and wiped out most of the rest of the remaining indigenous population. In a final act of revenge the local population destroyed the returnees' ship and with it their last hope of Space flight and escape."

"So," as the exobiologist explained, "what we have here is a planet now populated by the descendants of those who had returned from Earth, and the few original survivors of Keppler now stuck somewhere at the level of the Mayan civilization in the early 1500s. Biologically they are us, originally they are us, and they're all living together peacefully and harmoniously.

"A wonderful story, very uplifting," replied the commander of the Conquistadores.

"So what do they want?" he asked.

"Simply to be left alone, and grow in their own way," replied one of the exobiologists.

"You know that can't happen," replied the commander. "Discovery has happened and history always repeats itself."

"Operation Hernan Cortes is now under way," continued the commander, as two further drop ships began to land, both filled with heavily armed Conquistadores. "You know that this is for the good of Earth. We can't have a civilization that could eventually threaten the security of our planet continue to exist."

So for the second time in galactic history, the civilization known as the Mayan Civilization on Earth, and the Nuevo New Mexican Mayans of Keppler 1649-c, disappeared.

"Good job," said the Mission Commander of "Operation Hernan Cortes" to his officers and crew. "That threat's removed; now let's go find those Aliens who built the Egyptian pyramids."

The Mask of a Faun

Dramatis Personae

Gods, Deities and Heroes

Ajaxes: A pair of Greek Heroes who fought at Troy; Ajax the Great was a close friend of Achilles; Ajax the Lesser was the brighter of the two. Reports of their death after the Trojan War have been greatly exaggerated. Currently providing security for Asherah (see below).

Aphrodite: Olympian Goddess of Love, Passion and Beauty, previously caught in flagrante with Ares by her husband Vulcan aka "The Mechanic".

Ares: Bottle Blond now retired Olympian God of War, aka Victor Mars; Ares has now diversified into antiquities and is currently seeking to recover the Mask of a Faun and other Treasures, for an interested but unknown party. Previously caught in flagrante with Aphrodite by her husband Vulcan. Sworn off alcohol for the last 2750 years.

Asherah: A very old Babylonian goddess known as the "Lady of the Sea"; has lived on the Mediterranean Coast for many, many years. Owns a luxury block of flats on the slopes of Mount Carmel in Haifa, owns some real estate and runs a couple of Casino Cruise Ships in the Eastern Mediterranean. She is also a Cousin of Nergal.

Edesia: Roman Goddess of Food and Banquets. Has been the partner of Asherah for the last two millennia.

Hermes: Herald of the Gods but has now diversified into fashion and delivery services. Had a long-standing fling with Eriboea the stepmother of Otus and Ephialtes, ... Two lame-brain Giants who like to get drunk.

Minerva: aka Athena, Goddess of Wisdom and patron of the arts, now runs a very exclusive boutique in Paris with Diana, (as Artemis is now calling herself), and they now plan to open a branch in Knightsbridge. Together with the Egyptian God Thoth cast a spell to prevent all the Gods, and minor deities from being able to physically enter Museums, Galleries or Private Collections.

Minor Aesir: Minor Norse Deities who provide legal, maintenance and secretarial facilities to Nergal's "Deity Consulting and Investigative Service".

The Morrigans: Three Irish sisters previously known as the "Three Morrigna", associated with War, Fate, and Victory. Their emblem is a crow. They love to party. Now provide security for Nergal and his associates.

Nergal: Now known as Nigel E. Phrates – A Retired Babylonian God of War, now runs a bespoke "Deity Consulting and Investigative Service" from his offices in Lower John Street, Soho, London W1. Wears his long blond hair in the "lion mane" style.

Orcus: Roman God of Death and Broken Promises; often referred to as Pluto, Hell or Hades, an extremely powerful god with strong ties to Organized Crime, notably associated with the New York Five Families and is now based in Long Island, NY.

Otus and Ephialtes: Two lamebrain giants who like to get drunk; their young very attractive Stepmother Eriboea had a "thing" with Hermes.

Psecas: A Greek nymph who styled the hair of the Greek Gods and Goddesses. Left Olympus in a hurry two millennia ago and has lived in the UK since the Georgian era. Known as the Patron of Greek Hairdressers. Nowadays she runs a salon called The Gordian Knot, just round the corner from Fortnum and Mason's in Jermyn Street.

The Persian Immortals: Originally heavily armed elite infantrymen of the Persian Empire. Some have diversified into personal protection squads for Russian Oligarchs and other wealthy individuals.

Rhapsody: Previously known as Rhapso, a minor goddess and patron of seamstresses, runs a small-bespoke outfitter in Saville Row.

Salvatore: Legal Adviser to the Mafia Commission, and often represents senior members of the New York Five Families. Last name unknown. May or may not be the God Mendacius, (the God of Fraud and Deception); when asked replies "No Comment"

Sothis: Also known as Seshat, the "Mistress of the House of Books", always depicted wearing a Leopard Skin. Nowadays works for Nergal as an Archivist and lives just outside Billericay in Essex. Drives an old Jaguar E type – what else! Happily Married to Thoth (see below).

Thoth: The old Egyptian God of writing, wisdom and magic. A powerful God in his own right, loves tinkering with cars and drives an old Triumph Stag; and like his wife works for Nergal as an archivist. Together with Athena (Minerva) cast a spell to prevent all the Gods, and minor deities from being able to enter Museums, Galleries or Private Collections.

The Nine Muses: Nine sisters all daughters of Zeus, were minor gods who inspired artists, musicians and writers to be creative. Nowadays they've formed the girl group "FIVE GIR7S" and a management and recording company, and continue to inspire creativity in the arts.

The Valkyrie: The six Valkyrie choose the fallen warriors for entry into Valhalla. They were also very capable warriors both off and on the battlefield. Some have signed contracts with Hollywood to provide security and act as extras in various films.

Vulcan: aka "The Mechanic" now living in self-imposed exile in the Volcano on Fogo in Cape Verde. He plays no part in this adventure.

Zeus: The Senior Olympian and has far too many children. Has organised the move of the Olympians to London and currently holds an advisory position to the British Government. Because of his Olympian accent calls himself a "Spud" rather than a SpAd. Attends the Government meetings dressed in his wide brimmed hat, a gold trimmed Chiton, and a simple over the shoulder cloak. His hair and neatly trimmed beard are maintained by Psecas at her salon in Jermyn Street.

Some Real Stuff

Eisatzstab Reichsleiter: Known as Reichsleiter Rosenberg Taskforce. A thieving bunch of Nazis formed into an art squad in 1940 by Alfred Rosenberg, Head of the Nazi Political Office, and active throughout the war. Stole Art and whole libraries from national museums, galleries, and private collections all over Europe.

Fat Hermann: Aka Hermann Goering, A very, very fat man who was head of the Luftwaffe, President of Prussia, and Deputy Fuhrer. Stole artwork across Europe for his personal gain. Tried and found guilty of War Crimes at the end of the war.

Hermann Goering Panzer Division: Originally Hermann Goering's armed personal bodyguard; the division fought in Italy as part of the German 10th Army. In 1943-44 were notorious for stealing Italian works of art on behalf of their boss Fat Hermann, clearly yet another thieving bunch of Nazis.

Smiling Albert: Albert Kesselring – Generalfeldmarschall and commander of all German Forces in Italy during the Italian campaign 1943-44. Accused of War Crimes at the end of WW2.

The Real Real Stuff

"The Mask of a Faun" was displayed in the Bargello Museum in Florence, Italy until World War II when it was taken to Castello di Poppi for safekeeping. Between August 22nd and 23rd of 1944, German soldiers of the 305th division stole the artworks hidden in the castle. No trace of the mask was ever found.

305th Infantry Division: reformed in 1943 (the original Division had been destroyed at Stalingrad), mainly with the Sudeten Germans. Based around Rimini in late 1944 as part of the German 10th Army. Its Sister Division (278th Infantry Division) held the hills on the Sammarinese border. Men of the 305th Division are believed to be associated with the theft of the "Mask of a Faun" and other pieces of art that have never been recovered.

141

Sayaret Battalion: Literally "Reconnaissance Unit" specializing in intelligence gathering, surveillance and other Special Forces roles.

Chapter I

Nigel E. Phrates, the now retired Babylonian God of War and Death, had been around for a very, very long time, but had only set up his Security Consulting Practice in the mid-1960s in a new London that had overturned the bleakness of the last war.

The City at that time was buzzing with nightclubs, bars, fashion shops full of mini-skirted women; and someone had even come up with the phrase "Swinging London".

He had opened up his office in Lower John Street just back from Regent Street in an area that had over the years become increasingly fashionable and expensive.

Nigel had seen cities come and go, he'd witnessed the rise and fall of Babylon, Greece and Rome, and had fought in the Persian Invasion of Greece, The Crusades, Hundred Years War and more recently in the First World War. Now tired, worn out and dissatisfied with going to war, he had decided to provide a Deity Consulting and Investigative Service to the many Old Gods who were having to move away from their ancient homes due to the pressures of the Modern World.

Over the last fifty years he had helped relocate the Norse Gods to the North West region of Canada; the Roman Gods who'd been unfairly targeted by the Red Brigade had been moved to Long Island, New York, where their protection was guaranteed by the so called Five "Mafia" Families.

Many of the Hindu Gods he'd moved to the English Midlands where they had involved themselves in golf clubs and restaurants, and had bought a number of local football clubs.

Most of the old Egyptian Gods had long disappeared – they were Aliens anyway – and he presumed that those that had left had returned to whatever planet they'd originated from.

There was no doubt in his mind that his most difficult job to date had been negotiating the move of the Chinese Gods to Australia at the outset of the Cultural Revolution in 1966.

His original single office had now expanded, and over the decades he'd been able to acquire the whole building to fully accommodate his staff of mainly Minor Aesir, a couple of Valkyrie, and a number of Celtic Gods, together with his ever-expanding archives.

He'd been lucky to discover that the old Egyptian Goddess Sothis and her husband Thoth had stayed on Earth, and had been working for the Library of Congress in Washington ever since its opening in 1800. He'd persuaded them to join him, and they had now settled in as archivists, loving life in London, and Sothis was now living just outside Billericay and had even gone "All Essex" wearing Leopard prints at every opportunity.

Sitting in his brightly lit office, he was immaculately dressed in a handmade suit, his long blonde hair perfectly coiffed into a "lion's mane" style, and considering his next project; the location of the lost Mayan Gods, rumoured to be living deep within the Amazon Rainforest.

The tall handsome dark-haired man who was shown in by his secretary had a familiarity about him, but Nigel could not quite put his finger on why he thought he should know him. The secretary introduced the stranger as a Mr Victor

Mars, asked if both wanted tea or coffee, and quietly left the room.

"Of course," stated Nigel, "it's Ares isn't it? I haven't seen you in a millennium or two. I was fooled by the dark hair as I recall you had long blond hair last time our paths crossed; when was it? Around the time of Xerxes defeat in Greece or later during the Crusades? I forget. So many wars, so many battles."

"Good to see you, Nergal," Ares replied, addressing the clearly retired "God of War and Death" by his old Babylonian name.

"Yes, it was, just after the Persian defeat at Salamis, but I'm sure I caught a glimpse of you at that fiasco at Acre. I was with the Templars at the time, and we snuck out with the Templar treasure via those tunnels. As for the blond hair – the Greeks liked their male gods to be blond not dark, so it was all out of a bottle I'm afraid."

They paused their conversation whilst the secretary re-entered with a tray of coffee, cups, glasses and a bottle of Remy Martin XO cognac.

Pouring out the coffee and brandy, Nigel, or Nergal as he'll now be officially called, replied, "Yup, I was there, but I've hung up the God of Death and War mantle and as you can see I'm now providing a "Bespoke Deity Consulting and Investigative Service". What about you? What are you up to nowadays?"

"Thanks," said Ares. "I'll take the coffee but no brandy; I'm off alcohol. It's a long, long story, but thanks anyway."

Taking a sip of brandy and sitting back in his leather chair, Nergal continued, "I hear your boss is moving all of you away from Olympus; the rumours are that you're all coming here to London. Will you be requiring my relocation services, or is there something else I can help you with? Let me think – is it the Templar Treasure that you mentioned, the missing Golden Fleece? Or do you need my help in tracking down a lost God or two? Over the millennia I've built up extensive files on lost and missing deities, ancient and biblical artefacts and scrolls. As I've said, we can help with a discrete relocation service with all the necessary security, which can be provided by members of the Persian Immortals or selected warriors from Valhalla."

"Thanks. You're right about the move," replied Ares, "but that's more about the politico-economic problems in the EU than security concerns; and with the UK leaving, we feel that here is a better and less restrictive place to live. The UK government is being very supportive; Zeus has even been offered an advisory role to the British government. He's what they call a SpAd, a Special Advisor to the Government. He's also made quite a splash with his mode of dress; he insists on a gold trimmed Chiton, wide-brimmed hat and a simple over the shoulder cloak."

Looking at the old Babylonian God of War he grinned and continued, "Love the hair by the way. You must tell me where you get it styled. Sorry I digress, and yes, I do need your help."

"What with your hair?" asked Nergal. "My hair is done by Psecas. She's one of your lot, a Greek nymph I believe; been here for a couple of centuries, styled all those Georgian wigs for a while. Nowadays she runs a salon called *The Gordian Knot* on Jermyn Street, just round the corner from Fortnum's."

"No, no, it's not about the hair at the moment," answered Ares, "though that's interesting about Psecas; I wondered what happened to her. She used to do Aphrodite's hair, but disappeared a couple of millennia ago. I must pay her a visit sometime.

"Anyway, to continue; the reason I'm here is to ask for your help in specifically locating Michelangelo's *Mask of a Faun* which disappeared in Italy in 1944. I've been asked by an interested party to see if I could locate it on behalf of their client.

"Who's the interested party and why you in particular?" asked Nergal.

"Well Minerva, myself and the Nine Muses did help the French, Greek and Italian Governments repatriate many of their artefacts stolen by the Nazis at the end of the war in '45, though quite a few still remain missing, including paintings by Titian, Botticelli and Caravaggio, but most notably this particular item."

"Well, as for the interested party," Ares continued, "He goes by the name of Salvatore – just Salvatore, no last name, but I think you and I may very well know him as Mendacius; you remember he was supposedly the God of Fraud and Deception. He's currently an attorney and mainly does work for the Five Families and Mafia Commission in New York; used to be very tight with lot of very, very bad gods in the old days. I suspect that he's now acting for one of them. Won't tell me anything more than that, just that he's acting for an "interested party". Ask him anything more, and he just says "No Comment".

"That Mask is the first piece ever created by Michelangelo, and is supposedly based upon the true image of the god Orcus; you remember him the old Roman God of Death and Broken Promises, ugly old bugger.

"By the way do you mind if I smoke?'

"Not at all," said Nergal, pushing an ashtray across the desk.

Lighting up and taking a deep draw, Ares continued with his story. "Pound to a penny, this Salvatore's acting on behalf of Orcus, a very, very bad dude. You remember Orcus, moved around with a lot of other really bad guys back in the old days, Gods like Loki, Khaos, Phobos, and

Deimos. The word on the street is that they are now heavily involved in Organized Crime, but that's just the rumour.

"Anyway, what is known is that the Mask, and many other works were supposedly stolen by a bunch of German soldiers sometime in late August 1944, from the Castello di Poppi, where artworks from the Uffizi and Bargello Museums were being stored. We know that these stolen pieces were loaded on to a number of German Army Trucks, and then supposedly driven North away from the advancing Allies." Ares took a sip of his coffee, then resumed his tale. "After a brief stop in the little town of Forlì, the trucks containing these works of art supposedly continued northwards and thereafter the trail goes completely cold, and the Mask and other pieces seem to have vanished off the face of the Earth."

He reached into an inside pocket of his jacket and took out a printed sheet. "This is taken from the *US National Archives* detailing lost and looted World War II Treasures."

Ares read from the printed page. *"The Mask of a Faun* was displayed in the Bargello Museum in Florence, Italy until World War II when it was taken to Castello di Poppi for safekeeping. Between August 22nd and 23rd of 1944, German soldiers of the 305th division stole the artworks hidden in the castle. No trace of the *Mask* has ever been found."

Ares passed the printed sheet over to Nergal who quickly scanned it.

"Interesting," replied Nergal. "This report specifically states that the *Mask* was stolen by men from the 305th Division which is a good starting point; by the way whatever happened to Minerva and the Nine Muses?" he asked, sipping his coffee.

"Well." Ares stubbed out his cigarette. "Minerva opened a very select boutique in Paris with Diana, as

147

Artemis is now calling herself, and they're now looking at sites in Knightsbridge to open a second branch, what with our imminent move to London. The Nine Muses went into the music business, five of them have formed a girl group called simply FIVE GIR7S, and the other four, write, produce and manage the group."

Ares continued, smiling, "But that about sums up what is known about the fate of the *Mask* and those other artworks. All leads have gone dead, so your help would be much appreciated."

Chapter II

The Major and his platoon of Sudeten Germans knew the war was lost, and returning home was becoming increasingly unlikely, especially as the Russians were now poised to enter Germany. To the west the Allies were racing across France, and to the south were rapidly advancing up the leg of Italy, despite Smiling Albert's best efforts. Their prospects looked bleak: fight, surrender or somehow flee, but where to? The future would probably be ending up in a POW camp for who knows how long, with little prospect of going home, wherever that may be.

"Interesting", said Nergal. "Italy 1944, it was utter confusion at that time."

"OK let's go look at my files, they're all stored in the basement. I suppose like me as an old God of War you've accumulated records and details of all the major and many minor conflicts throughout history, though with help from Sothis and Thoth we've now managed to digitally store most of this stuff on computer."

"Nah, not at all," replied Ares. "Zeus was never a fan of computers. He insisted that if we had to look up old stuff we had to go and ask The Three Fates or even Father Chronos – "Getting the chronology" he used to call it!"

Ares followed his host as they descended the stairs to the basement.

He stared in speechless wonder at the huge brightly lit office filled with ordered files, multiple computer terminals and screens, and an extensive library of ancient texts – books, ancient scrolls, and stone tablets, many carefully stored under glass, and there in the centre of the room lit up by spotlights and protected by a glass case was Nergal's old War Mace, clearly a nod to his past life.

"OK" said Nergal, "pull up a chair. He seated himself in front of a computer terminal with a large overhead screen. "What other information do you have, if any?"

"Nothing much more, except the date when the *Mask* was stolen and the report that the German Soldiers that supposedly stole the *Mask* were just those men from the 305th Infantry Division, one of the divisions of the German 10th Army."

The men of the 1st platoon, 305th Reconnaissance Company had driven eastward from Florence to Poppi entering the town from the South. Major Hauptmann ordered the three trucks to halt in the piazza in front of the castle. Supposedly medieval it had been partly rebuilt in the 19th century so the façade was relatively modern. The castle was deserted, and surrounding town appeared to be empty of German soldiers, but the major had one thing and one thing only on his mind. Ordering the heavy machine gun squad to form a defensive perimeter, he took the first and second squads into the castle and down into its cellars. Here packed in a carefully ordered manner were artworks, sculptures and other treasures from the Uffizi and Bargello Museums that had been stored in secrecy under the very noses of the German. Amazing. Those idiots from the Hermann Goering have completely missed this. Consulting his notebook, he quickly organised his men to seek out a number of pieces of art by the Great Italian Masters and a number of lesser known painters plus his particular favourite the little known Mask of a Faun by Michelangelo.

"OK, OK, let's go." He quickly and quietly led his men back to the trucks, loaded up the three lorries and drove out of Poppi, crossing the River Arno by the last remaining bridge heading eastward.

"Men of the 305th, that's an interesting point," said Nergal. "Makes it much more likely that it was a heist, and not an officially sanctioned removal or theft of artwork. So I guess those guys were always going to disappear and sell whatever stolen items they could. They would have tried to avoid other military units, roadblocks and the Military Police." He pulled up a map of the region, then continued, "Personally, I don't think they would have driven north. Look, its more likely they would have driven eastward to nearby San Marino which during the conflict was a Neutral State, and was allowing refugees to enter." He searched on his computer screens. "The military records show that for a short period of time, members of the 10th Army were holding the hills on the San Marino-Italian border to the East, but were very rapidly overrun, and the City State was temporarily occupied by Allied Troops in Mid-September 1944, but only for a few days. So, if those guys did make it there, they would have remained undisturbed for the rest of the war – makes sense doesn't it?"

The major knew that whilst their own division was based further north in Rimini, their sister division was located

150

to the East of San Marino holding the hills that overlooked the route to Rimini. Additionally, he held orders that instructed the reconnaissance company to seek out likely artillery positions for the Division, so the movement of the three trucks all with markings of the 10th Army would not be hindered by either roadblocks or by the Military Police. Crossing into the declared neutral state of San Marino could be an option, and maybe, just maybe they could sit out the rest of the war in the Sammarinese State, whilst not in luxury at least in safety.

"Look, as Gods can't we just travel to back to August 1944 and lift the *Mask* from those German soldiers? Wouldn't that be easier?" asked Ares.

"Yes, it would be easier," replied Nergal, "but you know we can't, according to the UN Accord of the Gods Charter; the penalties are extremely severe for any interference in the past. We'll be hunted by Titans, Frost and Fire Giants, plus whatever nightmare creatures the Senior Gods, UN and World Leaders can think of, as everybody is worried about the Butterfly Effect. I know, I know that in late 1944 it's highly unlikely that anything would be changed, given the state of the conflict, but who knows what effect our interference could have, so we have to, and we will do it, the old-fashioned way."

Ares watched as Nergal worked on his computer terminal, muttering under his breath, "Interesting... very, very, interesting," as he pulled up various records, war diaries, photographs and military maps.

"OK," Nergal finally announced. "I think we've found the start of the robbery; I can probably figure out the middle and we have to solve the final bit, which hopefully is the nugget of Gold."

Looking at the computer screen and various displays he

continued. "The war diaries of the 305th indicate that a platoon from their Reconnaissance Battalion had been given orders to seek out suitable sites for artillery emplacements for the division, so they would've had wide ranging travel permits that would have got them through the various military roadblocks."

Nergal continued, "So, what we now know, is that the guys who probably did the robbery were likely to be these members of a platoon from the reconnaissance battalion of the 305th Division, which was made up of Sudeten Germans, so they could probably pass themselves off as Czech if the going got tough. The available personnel records – you know that the Germans were always so very efficient in their record keeping – indicate that the Battalion Commander was a certain Major Herr Professor Dr. Hauptmann, who'd been a Professor of Fine Art in the German University in Prague in 1939-40."

Chapter III

The major thought back to the summer of 1940 when two men from the Foreign Office had visited him, politely requesting that he accompany them to Paris to help assess some paintings that had been seized by members of the German Army Secret Field Police. A letter signed by Alfred Rosenberg, Head of the Nazi Party Political Office, had underlined the "polite request" and additionally confirmed a temporary rank of "Haupt-Einsatzführer" in a new unit called the "Einsatzstab Reichsleiter Rosenberg". The unit had been formed to catalogue and safely transport all forms of artwork for safekeeping in Germany.

He'd spent the next few months in Paris cataloguing Old Masters and works by Renaissance artists in various collections for what he supposed was their transfer for safe keeping to the Fatherland. Too late he realised that these artworks were being stolen for the private collections of senior members of the Nazi Party. In July 1941 he requested a transfer to a Panzer Division on the new Eastern Front. Over the next three years he would occasionally hear about members of the "Einsatzstab Reichsleiter" stealing works of art often with the blessing and support from Hermann Goering, the Deputy Leader of Nazi Germany. By the time he arrived in Italy in late 1943 now as a Battalion commander in a newly reformed Infantry Division, he was fully aware of the multiple art thefts being carried out in Italy by men of The Hermann Goering Panzer Division.

"The war diaries indicate that the platoon travelled with three trucks all marked with the insignia of their parent 10th Army. I have no doubt that our Herr Professor Doktor knew exactly what he was looking for, as did his men, and again I'm in no doubt that following the theft – which was more extensive than the records state, as some items have been recovered – the plan would always have been to head to San Marino."

"Well, well, well here's an interesting link from both the *Bundesarchiv* and *US National Archives,* and is probably another bit of confirmatory evidence. It concerns the recovery of the *Vase of Flowers*, a piece by Jan van Huysum. Apparently, sometime in late 1945, a German Soldier sent the piece to his wife in Germany from San Marino; with the suggestion that it would look good in a gold frame!"

"This particular painting was one of the many pieces that had been stored in the Castello di Poppi for safekeeping; so now we know that in late '45, at least one, but I suspect most of the platoon was still in Italy. I've accessed the various records and it seems that the wife is long deceased as is the husband who died in 1956. We do know that he returned to Germany in late 1946 claiming to have been a POW of the Allies. We might try and visit his children if we run out of leads."

The major and his men drove their three trucks onward to San Marino, the art treasures stowed in ammunition crates. With the ever-present allied planes ready to pounce on any German traffic during the daylight hours, they travelled by night without lights, and hiding the trucks during the day in various farm buildings along the route.

The Divisional Passes and written Orders allowed them to pass through the numerous roadblocks, and after four days of travel they finally crossed into the Republic of San Marino. Surprisingly both, members of the Sammarinese Gendarmerie and the German Military Police now manned the Republic's border post. A Feld gendarmerie sergeant, nodded to the major saying, "They've set up the Divisional HQ at the Grand Hotel; we're trying to respect their neutrality but also expecting the Amis any day now."

Entering the city proper, the major ordered one of the platoon sergeants who, having been brought up in South Tyrol, spoke fluent Italian, and two men, to seek out some garage space suitable for the three trucks, which they now parked up in the Piazza Della Libertà, the main square in the City.

The major and his men sat by their trucks, brewing their coffee, smoking and eating the remains of their rations, savouring the peace of the city. They could hear the sound of artillery far off to the south and east as the Allies continued their advance and enjoyed not having to run or hide from the overflying aircraft – a bizarre moment here in this Neutral City State.

"So," replied Ares, "you think our next step is to head to San Marino to see if we can trace their onward journey and then possibly on to Germany to speak to those relatives you mentioned, unless you have any other ideas?"

"Well, and it's only a supposition, I don't think many would have chosen to return to Czechoslovakia, which in the immediate post war years had an Ultra-Nationalist Government until the Communist Coup of '48. Those Sudeten Germans would not have been particularly welcome in either East or West Germany, so I think they would have left San Marino and Italy probably by boat, but where would they have gone?"

Nergal continued, "Let's see. They wouldn't have wanted to travel far, so a sailing from one of the nearby ports of Ancona, Rimini, or Ravenna would be the preferred choice, but where would they go? I know it sounds crazy, but I think they would have headed to the British Mandate of Palestine probably via Cyprus or they may have headed to Syria or Lebanon, but I think the Mandate would have suited them better."

"OK," asked Ares, "why there, and why not stay in San Marino?"

The sergeant had found a suitable place to secure and hide the trucks, and the major gathered his men around him. "We're now safe in San Marino, it's neutral and we can sit out the war. Those who wish to return to the war can leave, but we have a future stored in the trucks. What awaits us back home I don't know, but the Amis and Ivans will want a reckoning, and don't forget what Heydrich and Frick did to the Czechs, so don't think we'll be

155

welcomed back, and there'll be no place for us in what remains of Germany. So, we'll stay here awhile until we can figure out where to go." He wasn't surprised when not a single member of the platoon expressed a desire to leave the safe haven of San Marino.

"Well," continued Nergal, "by 1946 Palestine was opening up to European refugees, despite British attempts to control the immigration. People landing were undocumented, able to adopt any name they wanted, and disappear into the Palestinian territory. By the end of 1947 the Mandate was effectively at an end. Surprisingly at the end of the war San Marino voted in a Communist Government that pledged full co-operation with the Italian Government. In 1946 both Syria and Lebanon were still under the control of France, and they would not have tolerated a bunch of ex-German soldiers even if they were supposedly Czech, entering their territories. So, if they went anywhere it was probably to the Mandate and then who knows where?"

The war bypassed the major and his men. San Marino experienced a brief occupation by the Allies, essentially a four-day visit by the polite men of an Indian Division, and was then left completely alone. The City State had for a while experienced an influx of refugees, allowing the platoon to hide in plain sight, and by late 1945 the major and his men had become familiar faces in and around the city.

"OK. Think I've found it." Nergal smiled. "This is their route without a doubt. I had a fleeting memory of hearing about Czechs, Italy and the Mandate, and here it is. I'll call it *The Story of The Ship Called Dora*. Look, we've now got information on the sailing, crew, passengers and a cargo of three Trucks. The Italian freighter Dora sailed from the port of Ravenna in early March '46 to the Croatian port of Šibenik. Supposedly after berthing there for a week, the Dora sailed out into the Adriatic having taken on board "engine and agricultural parts bound for the port of Haifa".

In late 1945 the major had heard that Italian freighters had begun sailing from the nearby Adriatic ports to destinations in the Eastern Mediterranean, including Cyprus, the Levant, Turkey and Palestine. It took him three months to find a suitable freighter able to transport his men, the three trucks and their equipment to a destination that would suit their needs. The Italian captain of the Dora was willing, at a price which included protection at the next port of call in Croatia, to transport them to the Port of Haifa in Palestine. He assured them that entry restrictions were at a minimum, and the authorities usually turned a blind eye to the unloading of vehicles and engineering equipment. He was scheduled to pick up more cargo in Šibenik in Croatia and knowing how much hatred the Croatians had towards the Italians he would be grateful for the presence of a group of armed "Czechs" on board.

Nergal continued, and bringing up more data and consulting some old records and lists, he finally turned to Ares: "You can't argue with the old-fashioned registers and logs, so here we now have it in full. The Dora took two weeks to sail to Haifa from Šibenik, having run into problems with a storm in the Eastern Mediterranean, and had to shelter in Larnaca Bay in Cyprus. From there it appears she was escorted to the Port of Haifa by two British destroyers and berthed there on the 1st of April. There doesn't seem to be any information on the manifest, but it's

157

noted that a number of Czech engineers and advisors disembarked with their equipment, which we can assume are the trucks containing the stolen Art."

"That's amazing," said Ares. "Back in 1945 we got no further than acknowledging that the art stolen from the Castello del Poppi had disappeared without trace. We assumed that the stolen art had somehow got transported to either Germany or Switzerland, but here in less than a couple of hours you've managed to trace them to Haifa. We never even considered the possibility of San Marino, and we were right there in Italy, not a hundred miles from those pieces."

Ares peered over Nergal's shoulder at the open shipping logs. "Do we now head to Haifa, or have you any other suggestion?"

The port at Haifa was crowded with ships as the Dora docked, numerous people were disembarking from two large passenger ships, clearly refugees from Europe, and it was clear the port authorities were overwhelmed by the large number of arrivals. The trip had taken a couple of weeks including a stop in Cyprus as they'd sheltered from a violent storm. The last leg of the trip had included an escort by two ships of the Royal Navy, which the major thought was poetic justice.

"No," said Nergal, "we'll head out to Haifa. We can stay with my cousin Asherah, who's got a terrific penthouse flat that overlooks the bay and the city of Haifa. She's lived around the coast there like forever, well, back when the area was called Sycamine. Over the years she's been involved in the dye trade, housing the pilgrims visiting the area, and now owns some real estate and runs a couple of casino cruise ships working the Eastern Med. She knows or has known everyone in and around the area for the last millennium."

Chapter IV

Nergal continued, "OK we'll use the Citation, and fly out from City Airport direct to Haifa." He picked up a phone and spoke to his secretary. "We'll take Sothis, who'll love the beach, and can help with any archives we need to access, and the Morrigan Sisters to provide a bit of security; they deserve a break."

He put down the phone and turned to Ares. "OK we're all set to fly out this afternoon if that's good for you?"

"That's fine," said Ares, "but I'll need a change of clothes if we're going to scrabble around in Haifa. This suit is fine, but not ideal for the heat of the Mediterranean." He pointed to the dark blue pinstripe he was currently wearing.

"No problem whatsoever," replied Nergal. "What use is it being an Olympian if you can't work a minor miracle – at least within the boundaries of the UN charter?" He picked up the phone again.

"I'm sure you'll remember Rhapsody or Rhapso as she was known back in the day; she has a small exclusive bespoke outfitters just a couple of streets away in Saville Row. I'll ask her to pop across and measure you up for couple of suits, shirts etcetera and by the time we land in Haifa they'll be waiting for you; just call it the luck of the gods."

"OK, whilst Rhapsody is sorting out your wardrobe, I'll pack a few things and get the girls together and we'll head off to the airport in a couple of hours or so," said Nergal.

The Major and his men arranged for the offloading of their trucks and luggage now relabelled as agricultural machinery. The three Mercedes L3000 trucks had been stripped down, rebuilt and repainted in that green so often used by the British, and all insignias belonging to the German Army had been long discarded.

Of the original twenty-five men in the major's platoon, ten had left, with their comrade's blessing, in late 1945 to attempt a return to their home. Three had elected to stay in San Marino, and the remainder had chosen to stay with the major. Those men, who'd chosen to leave the platoon were each given one of the stolen pieces to do with as they wished.

Finally disembarked, the major and his men were grouped around their trucks and checking the maps of their new surroundings when they were approached by three men in military dress, bearing the insignia of this new young country.

They'd easily transited the airport; their Major Deity Passports, issued by the UN, ensured trouble free access through immigration and security, and they embarked on the private jet.

There was plenty of room on the jet, and whilst Sothis, dressed as always in a leopard-skin print, the three Morrigan Sisters and Nergal enjoyed their champagne, Ares stuck to water.

He'd sworn off alcohol many, many, years ago when he'd got roaring drunk with Otus and Ephialtes, a couple of lame-brained giants, who as a joke had chained him up and stuck him in a bronze urn. The only problem was that, those stupid giants forgot where they'd stored the urn, and it took almost forever for the Olympians to find him. If it weren't for the fact that his brother Hermes was having a "thing" with those idiot giants' young step-mum they'd never have found him. Oh well. The drinking had caused him huge problems, not least getting caught in flagrante with Aphrodite, and boy oh boy nobody had let him forget that one! Those Renaissance painters had been full of it: endless bloody paintings. They just wouldn't leave the subject alone! It's a pity the Nazis hadn't stolen and lost those paintings – he could've lived with that!

How long had he been now sober? About 2750 years but who's counting, so he sat back and sipped his water.

The Morrigans were getting drunker as the flight progressed. They'd finished the champagne and were now onto Guinness, but both Nergal and Ares knew that they'd sober up as soon as they landed. The three sisters were identical, in that they had the flaming red hair and green eyes typical of the Celtic warrior, and were all dressed in ripped skinny jeans and white T-shirts embroidered with a black crow.

After a smooth flight the Citation landed at the Uri Michaeli Airport in Haifa and taxied to the Private Arrivals Terminal, where the six disembarked. As they entered the cool, quiet air-conditioned Arrivals Lounge they were met by a small delegation of members of the Antiquities Authority, Public Security, Ministry of Defence, and Nergal's cousin Asherah.

The senior of the three officers approached the major and his men and said, "Gentlemen welcome to Palestine, and we know who you are, who you were, and why you're here. It's not been difficult to keep an eye on your progress from Italy. Nevertheless we have a proposal. We're a young country and in need of experienced men and trucks, but especially men with your military expertise. We'd like to offer you a role in our new army for the war that we know is coming. At present what you have in your trucks is of no concern to us; it doesn't represent theft from our people. We'd like you to help form and train a specialized Reconnaissance Unit. For this we'll provide new identities, citizenship and land for you and your men to settle down in this country. No further questions will be asked, and we'll protect you from prying eyes whoever they may be."

It took no more than a few minutes for the major and his remaining twelve men to nod their agreement.

In the departure lounge, the representatives from Public Security introduced themselves to Nergal and Ares, and Nergal confirmed that he, Ares, Sothis, and the Morrigan Sisters were merely on a social visit to the country and to seek out some clues regarding a number of missing antiquities.

The gentleman from the Antiquities Authority took Sothis aside and presented her with a number of photographs, gave her his card, shook hands and left.

"What was that about?" asked Nergal.

"They've found some new scrolls in some caves around the Dead Sea, and want me to take a look when we've finished up here. Will that be OK? Also, he tells me they've dug up some old personnel files from way back that should cover the period that we're looking at. They're incomplete, but they may help. I'll take a look at them tomorrow, then hit the beach with the sisters in the afternoon."

"That's fine," replied Nergal. He turned to Asherah. "OK, let's head over to the flat."

Two black Mercedes quietly drove the party to Ashera's block of luxury flats on the slopes of Mount Carmel and on entering the building Ares was pleased to see that the reception desk was manned by the two Ajaxes.

"Guys, great to see you. How long's it been? When was it? Outside the gates of Troy? What're you two doing here?"

"Oh, it's a long story," replied Ajax the Lesser. He was the brighter of the two. "But after Troy we never managed to get back home. Reports of our deaths have been grossly exaggerated. We shipped out with Odysseus – that was a laugh and a half, what with Sirens, Cyclops and all those other distractions. Anyway, we hit a bad storm near Anatolia and the two of us washed up on this coast. Asherah took us in, and we've been working for her ever since. How've you been?"

"Not bad, not bad," replied Ares. "Given up the drink, given up the war thing, got into antiquities, and hoping to find some stolen artefacts. How are you doing, Big Man?" He turned to Ajax the Great.

"All good," mumbled The Great. "It's been a bit quiet here for the last fifty years." He was always a man of action. "Can't complain. Life here is good. Miss Old Tenderfoot, though." He was referring to his old friend Achilles. "After that arrow, there was no way back from Elysium. Guess we'll eventually meet up sometime."

"OK, let's catch up when I've sorted out this problem with Nergal, and when and if Asherah can spare you guys," said Ares. He caught up with the rest of the party at the elevator as Ashera was telling the others about the flats.

As Ares joined them, she continued, "There are just two flats per floor, each with four bedrooms and two large verandas, all owned by various retired Babylonian and Phoenician Deities; you'll be able to catch up with many old friends," she said nodding to Nergal. "The Penthouse is very different. It occupies the top two floors, has six bedrooms, enough for all of you, and all-round balconies. I'll be staying in my other flat on the floor below."

Looking at Ares, she continued, "Hermes dropped by earlier and dropped off a number of packages for you from Rhapsody; some clothes I presume?"

"Are you going to need side arms or anything like that?" asked Asherah. "If so, the Ajaxes can sort you out from our armoury in one of the sub-basements."

"I don't think so," replied Nergal. "The sisters are all we need, with their particular gifts. Anyway, this is essentially a fact-finding visit, and we don't expect any problems."

Chapter V

Over the next two years the major and his men had formed and trained up a specialized reconnaissance battalion for the new army of the emerging state, and during the War of Independence the battalion successfully participated in the relief of the historic capital, opened the road to relieve the Second City and retook Haifa. By the end of 1948, Independence had been declared, and the new state was born. True to their word, the state provided them with new names and identities, citizenship and land to build on so they could settle down.

A couple of the major's men stayed on in the Defence Force helping the now renamed "Sayeret" Battalion develop into a Special Forces Brigade; the remainder, including the major, married local girls, settled down and built their houses on the land provided, though they remained a tight knit community. Locally they were known as the "Bohemians", and the area they lived in known as "Little Bohemia" though by the early 21st century the derivation of the name had been forgotten, as the area became increasingly gentrified by bearded hipsters.

After they settled into their rooms, the group met up in the vast living room that overlooked the city and bay, the city lights twinkling far below them.

Ares had been pleased to find that Hermes had delivered three new linen suits, midnight blue, grey and cream, all with bright red silk lining, a number of shirts and even some suede loafers. They were an exceptional fit. Rhapsody had really worked her magic.

He joined the party overlooking the city, just as food prepared by Asherah's partner Edesia was being served. As would be expected the food was superb, and Asherah asked Nergal what he was planning.

Briefly he ran through the account that he and Ares had uncovered, finishing with, "So what we're looking for is evidence that some seventy years ago a platoon of German-Czech soldiers having arrived here in Haifa, either settled here or moved further inland; we're trying to trace them or their descendants if there are any."

"I remember those boys arriving," said Asherah. "They called themselves Bohemian Czechs but most of us knew they were German soldiers from the Sudetenland; they helped out in the War of Independence and settled near here in the southern part of the city. There's an area called Little Bohemia where they built their houses and lived, but over the years many have died, and their families have probably sold up and moved away. Their leader was older than most of them, and I think he became a professor of Art History in the University of Haifa, though he passed away some years ago. I really don't know about his family or whether they're still around." She looked around. "Does that help?"

Nergal and Ares nodded in unison, and Nergal, turning to Sothis said, "Maybe you could somehow find out about the ownership of properties in this Little Bohemia, bearing in mind that they'll all have changed their names."

He turned to Asherah. "Do you recall the professor's name? I'm sure he's our missing major."

"Sorry," said Asherah, "I can't recall it."

"But I do," stammered Edesia, who'd been silent up to this point. "I did his farewell banquet when he retired from the university in the early eighties; I keep all my records in my office on the ground floor of this block."

"Brilliant, absolutely brilliant," replied Nergal. "If you can dig out his name, we can find out his original address, see what's happened to his property and whether there are any relatives still living there.

The subsequent years had been good for the major and his men. They'd all prospered; sure there was further conflict in 1956 and many of the men volunteered their services.

The stolen art remained untouched, locked away in the original ammunition boxes stored within the cellar of the major's house.

Some of those who'd returned to Germany eventually came out for a visit and spoke of a new vibrant West Germany, a grey unforgiving Czechoslovakia and an even worse country to the East.

The major, now renamed as Aaron Kaplan, began teaching the History of Art at the local institute, which eventually became a university and was one of the first professors appointed to the new department of Art History. He and his wife had a daughter who became a family doctor, and after her military service set up her practice in Haifa. The Major in his later years retrieved the Mask of a Faun which he hung in his study, and when questioned, merely called it an ugly piece of dubious vintage he'd come across in a local antiques market, but it was something he liked.

The major died peacefully in his sleep in 1989 aged eighty. He'd never ever told his family about the stolen art or the true origin of the mask. After his death, the surviving members of his platoon removed the stolen pieces of art and distributed them amongst themselves.

Some pieces they kept and others they arranged to be sold through a number of intermediaries. The Mask remained in its place in the Major's study.

The following morning Edesia checked her old records and proudly proclaimed, "The retiral banquet was held in June 1982 for a Professor Aaron Kaplan the first professor in Art History at Haifa University. He was a nice old guy, tall and straight, silver hair and spoke with a light Sudeten accent – a really cultured guy. The university and students really loved him, and as I recall there were a number of his friends who were also invited, all speaking with similar accents. They were all in their late sixties and early seventies."

"Well done, babe,' said Asherah. "That will help, won't it?" She looked at both Nergal and Ares.

"Outstanding," said Nergal. "Now we have to prove that this Professor Kaplan is actually our major and whether he, or his family or any of his friends have knowledge of the whereabouts of *The Mask*."

Following her father's death, the major's daughter moved back into the family home, but continued her practice in downtown Haifa. Her mother died some years later. The daughter, who'd married another doctor, again like her parents, had one daughter. Both doctors were killed in a car accident in 2015 and in turn their daughter, the major's granddaughter, moved back into the family home and completely remodelled the house in keeping with a twenty-first century design.

Sothis had tracked down the public and real estate records and confirmed that the major's granddaughter was now the owner of the property. She had also contacted the granddaughter and arranged for their party to visit the property that afternoon.

Nergal, Ares and Sothis pulled up in their air-conditioned

167

Mercedes. Ares was now smartly dressed in his new dark blue linen suit and crisply tailored white linen shirt and Nergal was similarly dressed; both exuded an aura of authority and strength. Sothis was, as one would expect, dressed in a leopard print dress, suitable for the afternoon heat on the Mediterranean.

The house was set back from the road in extensive grounds and in the terms of the real estate brochure would be described as: "A luxury villa nestled in the foothills of Mount Carmel with stunning views of the bay".

A slim fair-haired woman in her early thirties dressed in jeans and a white T-shirt, who appraised them with steely blue eyes, met them at the door.

Sothis, introduced herself: "Miss Shapira. We spoke this morning," and introduced the two men.

The woman replied, "Come in," and looking at Sothis said, "Love the dress; you must tell me where I can get a similar one. It looks terrific".

"Let me know your size and I'll get my friend Rhapsody, who makes all my clothes, to make one up for you; and as I said earlier these two gentlemen are interested in your grandfather and some of the artwork he may have collected over the years. They believe that he may have been in possession of an extremely rare piece that may have been made by Michelangelo. I don't suppose you have any idea of what may have happened to any of your grandfather's possessions?"

"Not really. I was only four when Grandfather died, and I remember that Mum and Dad cleared out Grandfather's study and other possessions when they took over the house. I must have been about ten when we moved back in. I do remember that when I used to visit him in his study there was a nasty looking mask he'd hung up over his desk. Its appearance used to scare me. Remember, I was only four at the time."

"Do you remember what happened to it?" Ares asked trying to contain his excitement.

"Sure," replied Abigail Shapira. "Mum hated it but Dad loved it, so they compromised and put it in the downstairs cloakroom, and to be truthful I don't particularly like it either, but when I had the house remodelled I kept it in the cloakroom, to remind me of Grandfather and my dad. Do you want to see it?

Nergal replied, "If it isn't too much trouble"

They both looked at the mask hanging in the cloakroom.

"That's it" said Ares. "That's Michelangelo's *Mask of a Faun*. I can't believe it, and that the major's family had no idea of its history or value; to them it's a just an ugly antique and a reminder of their beloved grandfather."

"OK," said Nergal, "now we've found it, I suppose you've now got to contact this Salvatore or Mendacius or whatever he's calling himself nowadays, so he can let his so called interested party know we've located this *Mask of a Faun*. What then? And why would they want the mask?"

"Not a clue," replied Ares. "Even if it was Orcus who was seeking the mask, to what end? I can't really see why they'd particularly want it anyway. A god didn't make it, so it'll have no particular powers, no magic or anything. We should just return it to the Bargello Museum, who was its original owner."

"Sure, but it's a bit more problematic than that, if as you say the interested party represents the New York Five Families, and they seem to want to obtain *The Mask* for their own purposes," replied Nergal.

"Maybe it does have something special about it," continued Nergal. "Michelangelo must have copied the image directly from Orcus himself, so maybe if Orcus has it in his possession it does have something what, shall we say unique about it, bit like my old Mace and your Spear."

"We should keep it out of his hands a little while longer; put it back in the Bargello Museum. The security is pretty tight in the museum and anyway you know the gods can't physically enter museums or galleries ever since Minerva or Athena, as she was calling herself then, together with Thoth put that curse on our entering those places all those years ago. Maybe you can just tell Salvatore that you couldn't locate it. What do you think?" asked Nergal.

"OK," answered Ares. "That might work. I'll give him a call." He took out his phone and dialled a number from his stored contacts.

"Ciao Salvatore," he said, as the man on the other end answered with the word "pronto".

"Bad news, I'm afraid, we've followed the trail from Italy but no luck; there's no mask, there are no more paintings, and we've now reached a dead end."

The line went dead at the other end.

"Oh well," said Ares. "What can they do anyway? Let's leave *The Mask*; it was a pleasure to see it. Let's get someone from the Antiquities Authority to pay the family a visit, and negotiate its return. Well at least to its rightful place."

Somewhere on the Amalfi coast, Salvatore, a tall muscular elderly man with a mane of white hair, who may or may not have been the God Mendacius, the Old God of Fraud and Deception, stared out to sea and put down his phone, having abruptly disconnected the call.

After a few moments he picked up the phone again, and made the call to New York. "Ciao Orcus," he said, speaking to the God of Death and Broken promises…

About the Author

Henry is a retired surgeon having worked for the NHS for over thirty-five years. He has in the past written and published a number of clinical and scientific papers, but began writing for fun following his retiral from clinical practice.

Henry mainly writes on a whole variety of topics: tales from the confused beginning of the universe, the modern day involvement of the Olympian Gods in London life, and a number of wartime short spy stories.

He has published a number of these stories on the *CaféLit* site and some have been included in *The Best of CaféLit*, and *Aftermath* published by Chapeltown Books.

He writes a monthly "Old Fogies" column for *The Edge*, a monthly magazine published in Chelmsford, and is a long term and avid supporter of Tottenham Hotspur.

Like to Read More Work Like This?

Then sign up to our mailing list and download our free collection of short stories, *Magnetism*. Sign up now to receive this free e-book and also to find out about all of our new publications and offers.

Sign up here:
  http://eepurl.com/gbpdVz

Please Leave a Review

Reviews are so important to writers. Please take the time to review this book. A couple of lines is fine.

Reviews help the book to become more visible to buyers. Retailers will promote books with multiple reviews.

This in turn helps us to sell more books... And then we can afford to publish more books like this one.

Leaving a review is very easy.

Go to https://amzn.to/3AVKyjV, scroll down the left-hand side of the Amazon page and click on the 'Write a customer review' button.

Other Publications by Bridge House

The Story Weaver
by Sally Zigmond

Story-telling has often been associated with weaving and
spinning. All is craft, cleverness and magic.

Here indeed we have a colourful mix of beautifully crafted
stories. Some are sad and others bring us hope. There are
tensions in relationships, fear of the unknown coupled with
surprising empathy, and accidents of birth. Death wishes are
reversed, sometimes but not always, and so are lives in other
realties. People's stories intersect as they wait for a bus. An old
cello causes havoc. A church clock always strikes twice… or
does it? Match-making goes wrong until it goes right. And so
much more.

"A wonderful collection of interesting tales. A real mixture
that will delight all readers." *(Amazon)*

Order from Amazon:

Paperback: ISBN 978-1-914199-54-7
eBook: ISBN 978-1-914199-55-4

The Adventures of Iris and Zach
by I.L. Green

Iris and Zach have an uneasy but intriguing run.

A vast patchwork landscape of life is displayed through stories relating both the wonder and absurdity we all recognize. With a focus on mental health, these stories take the reader from incarceration to freedom, fear to comfort. There are celebrations of life and poetic lows. The Yin and Yang aspects of life are recognized in new and deliberate examples that instil thoughtfulness and occasionally a smile.

Order from Amazon:

Paperback: ISBN 978-1-914199-34-9
eBook: ISBN 978-1-914199-35-6

A Gentle Nudge
by Mason Bushell

Stories to soothe your soul.

In a world drowning in negativity and dark events, we all need a little light and hope. With a little adventure, romance and even music, these short stories will give your hopes and dreams a nudge as they draw a smile.

A Gentle Nudge by Mason Bushell wraps you in calm.

Order from Amazon:

Paperback: ISBN 978-1-914199-42-4
eBook: ISBN 978-1-914199-43-1